Carissa Ann Lynch is the *USA Today* bestselling author of *My Sister is Missing*, the *Flocksdale Files* trilogy, *Horror High* series, *Searching for Sullivan*, *13*, *13: Deja Vu*, *Grayson's Ridge*, *Shattered Time*, *Things Only the Darkness Knows*, *Shades and Shadows*, and *This Is Not About Love*. She resides in Floyds Knobs, Indiana with her husband, children, and collection of books. Besides her family, her greatest love in life is books. Reading them, writing them, holding them, smelling them…well, you get the idea. She's always loved to read and never considered herself a 'writer' until a few years ago when she couldn't find a book to read and decided to try writing her own story. With a background in psychology, she's always been a little obsessed with the darker areas of the mind and social problems.

Read More from Carissa Ann Lynch
Join Carissa's mailing list: http://eepurl.com/chb46z
Facebook: https://www.facebook.com/CarissaAnnLynchauthor
Twitter: https://twitter.com/carissaannlynch
Amazon Author Page: http://www.amazon.com/
Carissa-Lynch/e/B00REPXXW6/
Website: https://carissaannlynch.com

# *Without A Trace*

## CARISSA ANN LYNCH

KILLER
READS

A division of HarperCollins*Publishers*
www.harpercollins.co.uk

*KillerReads*
an imprint of HarperCollins*Publishers* Ltd
1 London Bridge Street
London SE1 9GF

www.harpercollins.co.uk

This paperback edition 2019

First published in Great Britain in ebook format by HarperCollins*Publishers* 2019

A catalogue record for this book
is available from the British Library

ISBN: 9780008324513

Set in Minion by
Palimpsest Book Production Limited, Falkirk, Stirlingshire

Printed and bound by CPI Group (UK) Ltd, Croydon, CR0 4YY

*For Violet, my daughter*

*There is nothing I would not do for those who are really my friends. I have no notion of loving people by halves, it is not my nature.*

Jane Austen, *Northanger Abbey*

*I don't believe in ghosts. But standing here now, with the tips of my toes tingling with heat, and my eyes stinging, not from the fire but from me, forcing myself to keep them open, never blinking, I can't help wondering if she'll come back and haunt me for this. Her limbs twist at uneasy angles. Her skin splits apart and dissolves. Her hair and clothes fall away, like feathers caught in a dust storm. And her face…it almost looks plastic, quivering and bending in the amber glow of the flames. It's as though she never breathed life in the first place. This is not how I imagined it—I thought it would be quicker. I thought she would scream more. Fight more. But it's almost like she's resolute, like she's telling me it's okay…that she forgives me for what I must do.*

# CHAPTER ONE

*The Mother*

## NOVA

I shivered as I stepped off the front porch and followed the well-beaten path down to the shady tree line. It was early, the sun playing peek-a-boo through the trees, and little wet kisses of dew were sprinkled around the yard like watery pockets of glitter. Such a peaceful morning, like the promise of a brand-new day. A *beautiful* day, in fact.

It was a rental property, but still, it felt like mine. Like the perfect place to raise my daughter.

Suddenly, the wind whipped through the trees, shocking the breath from my chest. It reminded me of what I already knew—*looks can be deceiving.*

Clouds bubbled up in the sky, the morning sun dissolving away like a figment of my imagination. As a flurry of cold air rushed around me and through me, I pulled my jacket tight against my chest and glanced back at our new house. It was a small log cabin, like something you'd see at a state park or campground. But the size was perfect for the two of us, and unlike my husband, I liked the coziness and simplicity of a single-family home.

Lily would be waking up any second now, and I didn't want her to be afraid in our empty, new house.

*How can I raise a daughter who is strong and brave when I'm so damn scared all the time?*

I took one last look at the trees, at the once-soothing sunrise. Branches morphed into bony claws. They reached for me, gnarly and twisted, eager to pierce through my ragged flesh like broken bones…

Whipping around, I raced back toward the house. A low moan escaped from between my teeth as the house swayed from side to side, like one of those carnival mirrors. The distance between the front door and the tree line suddenly stretched, for what looked like miles…

My sneakers were squishy on the cool, wet grass, and as I slipped and slid across the yard, I imagined the mud was quick-sand, sucking me deep down into the earth, consuming me whole…

Once inside, I locked the door and pressed my back against it, sucking in long, craggy breaths until they evened out. It only took a few minutes to still my thumping heart.

*That's better. Well done, Nova,* I commended myself. Each time I panicked, it was taking fewer and fewer minutes to calm back down.

*Hell, maybe after a few weeks of being here, I won't have panic attacks at all.*

Fumbling for a light switch in the kitchen, I stubbed my toe on Lily's tiny *Cars* suitcase. It was still lying in the middle of the kitchen floor, next to my duffel bag, where we'd tossed our luggage last night.

In the light of day, our new kitchen looked different than it did last night. White paint on the cupboards looked yellowish and worn. The sink was rusty, and a slow drip of water *ping ping pinged* in the basin below. Looking around, I tried to imagine this kitchen as our own—baking cookies for Lily while she sat on the edge of the counter, kicking the backs of her heels against the cupboards below. Normally, I would make her get down because Martin didn't like that.

*But now Lily and I can do whatever we want.*

And a rundown, drippy kitchen was better than any sort of kitchen we might share with Martin.

A scarred wooden table with four chairs was set in the kitchen. There were other modest furnishings, too—a chair in the living room, beds and dressers in both bedrooms—which was one reason I chose this place. It was the perfect getaway spot, out in the middle of nowhere, and we didn't need to bring much to get started.

The refrigerator and cabinets were still empty and in need of a good scrubbing. We'd grabbed some fast food on the way to West Virginia, but I hadn't wanted to stop at the grocery store yet.

*All I wanted to do was get us here.*

But now that we were, I'd have to spend the weekend making it as homey and comfortable as possible for Lily.

*We're doing this. We're starting over. This is our home now.*

For months, *years*, I'd imagined this moment. But then, it had just been a fantasy, a twisted version of hyper-reality. I never really thought I would leave. Even the night before we left, I'd expected myself to back out. To freeze. To panic and collapse in the middle of the street after loading our cases. But I didn't. And it wasn't until we were almost a hundred miles outside of Granton that I knew it was really happening…that we were leaving Martin for good.

My duffel bag lay sprawled open on the floor beside the table, from where I'd taken out my pajamas last night. We were so tired when we got here, to the point of delirium. It had taken nearly ten hours to reach Northfolk, the rising hills and winding curves of West Virginia making me skittery and afraid. I couldn't stop checking the rearview mirror and my heart was thrumming in my ears the entire drive. During the daytime, it hadn't been so bad. But at night, I'd imagined every pair of headlights were the angry, glowing orbs of Martin's truck, chasing us up the wild, mountain roads...

Lily had handled the move so well, believing me when I told her that we were going on an adventure. With her mousy brown hair and cornflower blue eyes, she looked just like Martin. But, luckily, she hadn't inherited his meanness, or his wild mood swings.

Lily was, by all accounts, a normal four-year-old girl. But that wouldn't have lasted long, not while living with Martin. Eventually, his violence would have moved onto her, seeping into her pores and saturating her life with his poison.

She was innocent, so seemingly unaware, yet she'd already learned to fear her father and his unpredictable ways. And the way Martin looked at her...his eyes searching, evaluating her every move, it made me uneasy.

*I'm taking her away from her dad. What kind of mother does that?*

Emotions played tug-of-war inside me—I felt guilty for stripping her of her fatherly influence, but I was relieved—exuberant, even—to give her a fresh, safe start in life. During the drive to Northfolk, I'd been so focused on getting away, that the guilt hadn't had time to settle in yet. And last night, I'd been too tired to stay up worrying. But now...now all those worries came rushing back at once.

*What will I tell her when she's older? Surely, she will remember Martin. Will I tell her why we left? How much memory can a four-year-old retain?*

"I m-made the right decision," I told myself, firmly, for the hundredth time this morning.

Pressing my face against the window pane, my eyes scanned

the backyard. From behind a layer of murky glass, the branches no longer seemed murderous or threatening. Even the clouds were wimpy, less dark. It was ironic, really. After years of feeling claustrophobic, shut inside the house with Martin, now it was the outdoors that overwhelmed me.

*Everything overwhelms me.*

Again, my thought from earlier came crawling back: *how can I raise my daughter to be a stronger, better version of me when I'm so scared of the world and the men that live in it?*

Clutching the necklace at my throat, my fingers curled around the dainty silver cross that Martin had given me on our anniversary. The holy symbol should have brought me comfort, but all I could think about were his hands pressed against my throat, the crossbars digging sharply into my flesh as I struggled for a tiny bit of air…

Tenderly, I reached back and unclasped it. It seemed wrong to throw it away, but then again, I couldn't keep it. It hadn't protected me when I'd needed it to, and expelling Martin's memory from our lives was my top priority now. Before I could change my mind, I carried the lightweight pendant over to the waste basket and tossed it inside.

I didn't put on makeup this morning. There was no rushing around to make Martin's breakfast, or to see him off to work.

No slamming doors or missing shoes or screaming.

*No angry fists pummeling my body.*

Most mornings, the air felt suffocating and dense. I'd wake up panting, a surge of panic hammering through my bloodstream and lifting me from bed. I was always afraid I'd oversleep, and sometimes I did. If Martin was late for work or didn't have the things he needed in the mornings, he blamed it on me. And worst of all, he seemed to enjoy punishing me for my mistakes.

He must have been so angry when he realized we were gone. We didn't take much when we left, just Lily's suitcase and my bag. But he must have known immediately.

The first thing he probably did was call my cell phone, and from there, it wouldn't have taken him long to find where I'd left it—on the nightstand next to our bed.

*He can't reach us here.*

There was no note. No paper trails. I'd saved up small amounts of cash over the past year, so there wouldn't be any need for ATM withdrawals. I had enough money to last us for a while, until I could figure out how to get some more.

Pinching my eyes closed, I couldn't shake the image of his seething blue eyes, the angry caterpillar brows furrowing in anger.

*He's probably mad enough to kill me right now. To kill us both.*

I could almost taste his rage from six hundred miles away. It tickled the back of my throat and burned the edges of my tongue.

*Fear. I can taste that, too.*

The fear I'd felt earlier was rushing back. My old friend Panic seized my chest, like a boulder pressing down on my belly, making every breath tight and controlled.

*He might find us. What will I do if he does?*

As I passed through the hallway, fingertips grazing the unfamiliar walls of the cabin, I thought I heard a muffled grunt coming from behind Lily's closed bedroom door.

*Nonono. He's not in there. I'm only imagining he is.*

I'd imagined his voice last night, too, before I fell asleep. The angry, breathy snores that he made while he slept. My body so accustomed to sleeping next to his, I'd lain against the edge of the mattress, curled into a tight little ball, despite all the extra space.

"One, t-two, th-three…" I counted out loud.

I read somewhere that counting helps alleviate anxiety. My lips silently formed the words, but the clenching in my chest remained. Suddenly, I was hurtling back to our house in Tennessee. Fear slithered in through the logs. Martin's anger dissolving and sinking down through the rafters…

"F-four, f-five, six…" My skin tickled and crawled, my stutter rearing its head again, becoming worse, the way it always did when I sensed a confrontation coming. As I moved through the hallway, I fought the urge to look back over my shoulder.

*Martin is not standing behind me. He's not!* I chastised myself.

The hallway tilted and swayed, then slowly, the buttery yellow paint dissolved. I wasn't back home in Tennessee; I was in our new house, faraway from Martin.

*Safe.*

"A-are you a-awake yet, Bunny?" My stumbled words a mere whisper through the heavy door.

*Bunny.* It was a nickname given to her by Martin, and I'd have to remember to stop using it. It would only serve as a reminder of him, and Lily wouldn't need any of those, now that he was out of our lives for good.

Closing my eyes and taking a deep breath, I nudged the bedroom door open. Soft sunlight streamed in through moth-eaten curtains above the bed. There was no Martin.

*See? Nothing to be afraid of.*

Lily, so tiny, was curled up beneath the blankets in a ball, unmoving. Like me, she was always trying to make herself smaller and unseen...

Lily had never been a good sleeper. She was prone to nightmares, but last night, she'd slept all the way through. Reaching across the bed, I slid the curtains back, welcoming more light into the room. The bright white heat was soothing, like a warm cloth across my face. I released a long stream of breath, relieved.

"Rise and shine, B—" I stopped myself from using the nickname again, squeezing my lips together. There were so many bad habits to break, and this was only just one of them...

I prodded the soft little lump in the middle of the bed. But Lily didn't move a muscle.

Finally, I rolled the covers back, imagining her sweet morning smile and sleepy doe-like eyes.

*I know they say you should always love your children no matter what, and I do, but for some reason, my heart just soars when I see her doughy cheeks every morning. She is always at her sweetest when she first wakes up.*

"Lily?"

A strange wisp of gray-white hair poked out from beneath the blanket. I stared at it, my mind not comprehending the strange bit of fur.

Tentatively, I rolled the covers down. Button-eyes stared back at me, black and menacing.

It was a toy rabbit, but not like the ones Lily used to keep on her bed in Tennessee. This bunny looked ugly and old, its limp arms and legs adorned with black, plastic claws.

I poked at the strange stuffed toy, shaken.

"B-bunny? Where are you?" I grasped the corner of the blanket in one hand, then yanked it the rest of the way off.

Lily wasn't in her bed.

A deep guttural scream pierced the morning air.

# CHAPTER TWO

## *The Cop*

### ELLIE

It started with a phone call, buzzing on the bathroom sink as I painted my eyes with charcoal liner.

"Makeup? Is that wise?" My mother was leaning on the door-frame, watching me get ready for work. Even though she retired from teaching five years ago, she still got dressed up like she was going to work each morning. Today she was wearing a creamy, salmon-colored pantsuit with brown pumps and a string of pearls.

"Just stop, mom." I rolled my eyes, dusted off my right palm, then took the call. It was Sergeant DelGrande, so loud and brash my mom could probably hear his words clear as day, even if she hadn't been standing right by my side.

I mumbled 'yes' a few times, adjusting my thick brown pony-tail in the mirror as I balanced the phone between my shoulder and cheek. I hung up and tucked the phone in my back pocket.

"What was that about?" my mother clucked, pretending she hadn't heard.

"Nothing to worry over. See you at dinner." I kissed her on the cheek then hurried out the front door.

"Be safe," she added as I left, almost too quiet for me to hear.

As I climbed in my cruiser and buckled my seatbelt, she was perched like an eagle behind the curtains, keeping watch as I reversed down the driveway.

Most parents would be proud of their twenty-eight-year-old daughter who was just starting out in the police force, but Barbara James wasn't your usual mother. She was Catholic and came from a strict family, and she had tried to raise me much the same way.

When I told her I was taking the law enforcement entrance exam, she had laughed. But when I passed the test and entered the police academy, that laughter had turned to tears.

Not only was she worried because the job was dangerous, but she was also concerned about my reputation. *What will people in the parish think when they find out you want to be a cop?* she'd asked.

First off, I didn't give a damn about my mother's parish. Part of me relished the thought of their gaping faces when they learned about my new job.

Secondly, I'd reminded her that I didn't *want* to be a cop. *I am a cop now*, I'd told her. And there was nothing Barbara James, or anyone else in Northfolk, including the parish, could do about it.

I'd always been fascinated by people. I wanted to help them. *Understand them.* And as corny as it sounds, I wanted to make a difference in the world. At first, I'd considered psychology or social work. But what better way to make a difference than to help the one group of people that no one gives a damn about? The *incarcerated*.

But Eddyville Penitentiary was hours away, and it paid more to be a cop than a corrections officer. It started out as a small dream, but once I'd entered the academy, it became an obsession.

An obsession that, once upon a time, stretched beyond being a small-town cop in my tiny town of Northfolk...

But my views on helping and understanding criminals were looked down upon by my peers, and I was reminded at the academy, more than once, that it was my job to help the *community*, not the criminals who muck it up. I understood their point of view, but I was idealistic—couldn't I help the community *and* try to make a difference in people's lives? Was it really impossible to do both?

Northfolk was a close-knit mountain town, comprised of less than five thousand people. Nevertheless, it was riddled with poverty and with that came heavy drug problems, specifically heroin and meth. Besides drug crimes, sometimes I had to cite people for shooting off unregistered guns or riding ATVs on private property. Domestic disturbances and petty thefts occurred occasionally, too, but they were the exception, not the norm.

I'd only had one serious incident since joining the force, but it was enough to change all those well-thought-out plans I'd previously made. Four weeks into my new job, I'd been called to the scene of a domestic disturbance. I didn't recognize the red-faced, frazzled woman who opened the door, but I did recognize her husband. A well-known cop, Ezra Clark, was accused of assaulting his wife. I had no choice but to call it in...and to arrest him. But what happened next...well, let's just say that Ezra didn't take too kindly to a new, young, female cop trying to take him into custody. He was angry and drunk, and although the scuffle between us only lasted a few seconds, the results had caused long-term effects. Possibly, *lifetime* effects. Memories of that day came floating back...the pounding pop when I fired my own gun, the burning smell of gunpowder in my nose. On my lips...

Would I ever be able to forget that day? And most importantly, would my colleagues and the residents of Northfolk...?

Sergeant DelGrande's instructions circled back through my mind. He'd asked me to go directly to 8418 Sycamore Street, where a woman had called in, claiming that her ex-husband had stolen her child right out of bed. It sounded like a domestic disturbance, but I wasn't familiar with the address. It was near the old Appleton farm, but no one lived out there besides the Appletons, as far as I knew.

As I pulled down the gravel drive to the property, I was instantly met by a running woman. Thick black hair swept across her face, a silky pink robe blowing back like a cape in the wind. I closed my eyes, fighting back images of Mandy Clark opening the door that day...if I let myself think about it long enough, I could still remember the smoky smell of Officer Clark's flesh as I pulled the trigger...

The events of that day were still such a blur. One minute, I was sliding the cuffs on his wrists, and the next, it was me being slammed against the hood of my cruiser. *You think you're tough, don't you? You don't know shit, rookie.* He let me go, but then he did the unthinkable: he reached for my gun. Afterwards, my fellow officers would claim that Ezra was probably just teasing, trying to show me I was ill-prepared as a new cop...but he was wrong about that. When he reached so did I...and moments later, one of us was lying dead on the ground...

Cautiously, I parked and emerged from my patrol car. While most of my male colleagues would have itched their fingers over their guns at the sight of a hysterical person, my instinct was to go to her, to calm her down. She was clearly distraught, her cheeks streaked with tears, her skin blotchy. I couldn't shake off images of Mandy Clark's distraught face, her battered skin stretched over her face like a ghoulish mask...

"Sh-she's gone," the robed woman choked out the words, all the while fighting with the hair around her face. "M-my Lily's gone."

The wind howled, blistery cold for September, causing me to

stumble a bit with the heavy belt weighing down my mid-section. I shook off my whirling thoughts about that day with Ezra Clark and tried to focus. "Ma'am, let's go inside and talk. Would that be okay?"

She hesitated, giving me the once over as though I were a stranger asking to use her phone. Her eyes were wild, shell-shocked. Maybe she knows who I am. Maybe she knows I shot a colleague, I thought. But that's ridiculous, I chastised myself, immediately. This woman was new to Northfolk; she couldn't possibly know about the Clark incident.

"I'm here to help. You called *us*," I gently reminded her.

Shakily, she led the way inside. The cabin was sparsely furnished, a small arm chair and rug in the center of the living room. Everything looked worn but clean, and not recently used.

There was no TV, no pictures or personal effects.

"How long have you lived here?" Awkwardly, I tried to adjust my belt, then took out a notebook and pen from my back pocket. The pages were blank, which for some reason, made me feel embarrassed.

"I just moved in yesterday. Me and my daughter, Lily. She's f-four."

"And your name?"

"Nova Nesbitt." The words were like whispers, strained.

"And your ex-husband, how long have you two been divorced?"

Nova shifted from foot to foot, chewing on a stray piece of hair and looking around the room with those wide, wild eyes. "Well, we're not. I mean, I-I only just left him y-yesterday."

I clicked the bottom of my pen, open and closed. It was a nervous habit.

"Does he live in Northfolk, too?"

"No. He's b-back in G-Granton, Tennessee. I can g-give you the address though."

After I scribbled his name, address, and phone number down,

I closed my pad. "Ma'am, if you're not legally divorced and you both share custody of the girl, then it's not a crime for her to be with her father."

Nova was pacing now, her skimpy undergarments exposed as the robe shifted back and forth across her thighs. She was a tall woman, but painfully thin. I thought about that expression, the one about a stiff breath of wind blowing someone away.

She stopped moving, her face twisting with desperation as her eyes searched mine. "L-listen, you d-don't understand. He was abusive. He *is* abusive. That's w-why we left. I d-don't know how he knew we w-were here...he must have followed me! And w-while I was asleep, that bastard t-took my daughter. She's in d-danger. You have to b-believe me. Her life depends on it! He will hurt her to get to me, m-mark my w-words." It was painful watching her mouth twist and struggle to form the words.

"Do you have a restraining order against him?" Part of me was secretly glad he wasn't here. The thought of getting directly involved in another domestic dispute made me more uneasy than I'd like to admit.

Even though she was looking right at me, it seemed like Nova was seeing straight through me now. Her eyes turned smoggy and lost.

She mashed her hands down on her hips, and muttering under her breath, she said something about a piece of paper being unable to keep someone safe.

I could see her point but having a legal document that prevented her husband from taking the girl would have made my job much easier.

"Have you tried calling him?" I asked, unsure what my next move should be here. I had been so confident when I'd started this job—maybe too confident—but lately, I couldn't shake the feeling that I was like a little kid playing dress-up in my cop's uniform. After the incident with Ezra Clark, none of my colleagues trusted me or wanted to work with me…and lately, I'd found that I was struggling to trust myself…

Domestic situations were always tricky, and sometimes the parents used their kids as pawns, or weapons, to hurt each other. Was that what was going on here?

Nova shook her head. "I-I haven't c-called him." She reached for the arm of the sofa, stumbling to catch herself from collapsing to the floor below.

I kept my eyes on her as I flipped through a couple blank pages in my notebook. Still gripping the couch arm for dear life, she closed her eyes. She was muttering under her breath, counting, I think…

I was close enough to smell her breath and I noticed it was hot and stale. But I caught a whiff of something else, too. Alcohol crossed my mind, but this smelled more minty, possibly like mouthwash. Did she wash out her mouth with mouthwash before I came?

That didn't seem like something a distraught woman would do, I thought. But looking at Nova Nesbitt, there was no question in my mind: this woman was freaking out. She seemed scared. Skittish.

Scanning her face again, I looked for signs of drug use. Although heroin was the main drug of choice in these parts, I'd been around a lot of meth users, too.

She was acting strange, but her pupils were normal-sized. She didn't appear to be on drugs, but then again, it wasn't always easy to tell.

"He's d-dangerous," she repeated, rocking back and forth on her heels. "Very dangerous."

"Can I see where Lily was sleeping?"

Without answering, Nova drifted down a shadowy hallway, dragging her robe along like a bridal train. Cautiously, I followed behind, looking for anything out of order. We passed a master bedroom and bathroom. Both looked empty and pristine.

19

When we entered the child's room, I immediately noted that it was neat but bare, like the rest of the house. There was only a twin-sized bed and dresser in the room. The bed unmade, there was a creamy blue blanket folded neatly at the foot of it.

"Found this." Nova held up a strange, stuffed toy. I took it, turning it over and back in my hands. It was odd, unlike any sort of stuffed animal I'd played with as a girl. A rabbit, and a downright ugly one at that, with eerie button eyes and worn out brown fur. It had plastic black claws on its hands and feet and two jagged white teeth protruded from the bunny's mouth. There were a few pieces of gray string protruding from its head. It almost looked… cruel.

"Is this your daughter's toy?" I set the creepy rabbit back down.

Nova was pacing beside the child's bed. She stopped and threw up her hands in disgust. "No! Why aren't you listening? I found it! My husband…he calls Lily his 'little bunny'. I think he left this here to taunt me. He's dangerous! Please, you have to take me seriously!" In Nova's angry outburst, the stutter had all but disappeared.

The hairs on the back of my neck stood on end as I stared at the forlorn toy. *Little Bunny.* What a creepy thing to leave behind if he was the one who took her, I thought. Suddenly, this seemed less like a custody dispute, and more like a kidnapping…but the last time I got involved in a domestic squabble, a man had ended up dead. And my nickname by my colleagues—"Cop Killer"—ensued.

"I'm going to take a look around the rest of the house. That okay?"

"Yes! That's why I called you, isn't it?" Nova huffed. She walked out of the room, mumbling to herself again.

As I walked around the side of the bed, looking more closely at the room, I couldn't help but be reminded of playing hide and seek with my cousins and friends when I was a kid. Could Lily be hiding somewhere?

20

It was possible that the husband took her, but I hadn't seen any signs of struggle or forced entry. How did he sneak the girl out?

The window behind the bed was locked tight. I peeked beneath the bed. The wood floors were clean, no dust or debris underneath. Next, I checked out the closet and drawers. I was surprised to find them full. A neat row of children's clothes hung from the rack. Removing a pale-yellow dress, I was surprised to find it still had tags attached. I sifted through the other outfits too—everything looked brand new.

"Ms. Nesbitt?" When I stuck my head out of the bedroom, I was surprised to find her standing right there in the hall. As we came nose to nose, I jumped and made an embarrassing squeaking sound.

"F-find anything?" She gnawed on her nails, shifting from foot to foot, reminding me of a toddler waiting to pee.

"Did you buy new clothes for Lily?"

"Oh. Yes," Nova said, nodding. "We d-didn't have time to pack m-much."

I nodded, then resumed searching. The first two drawers were full of underwear and socks and the bottom drawer contained books and toys. Again, all looked brand new. Some were even wrapped in their packaging still.

Something about this whole thing felt off. I could understand having to buy new things when moving, but new *everything*? It seemed highly unusual.

Next, I walked through all the other rooms, checking for broken or unlocked windows. I opened closets and looked beneath the few furnishings inside the house.

A new thought was shifting around in my mind. "Lily wouldn't wander outside on her own, would she? New house, new place. Maybe she went off to explore?" Images of dead, floating kids in ponds fluttered through my brain. And miniature, mangled bodies by the side of the road, the bent-back limbs protruding…

21

I'd never seen any of those things in real life, but I'd seen plenty of ghastly images while studying at the academy. Some of the men in my class liked to "shock" me with them, sticking them in my locker and desk drawers during training. I was one of only two women in my class, and behind our backs, they liked to call us "the pretty one" and "the ugly one". I think I would have preferred the latter.

"No, she wouldn't. I s-sat on her bed, r-reading to her until she fell asleep. And I ch-checked on her a few times before I w-went to bed last night. I was w-worried. I looked around outside b-before I called, but I-I know h-he took her…"

"How do you think your ex got in the house, if he didn't have a key?" We were standing in the kitchen now. I stared at the child's suitcase on the floor. It was decorated with smiley red cars, the one from that Pixar movie but I couldn't remember the name of it. Not having a child myself, I suddenly felt unsure how to help this woman. My mother would know what to do and where to look, I thought. Instantly, I pushed that thought aside, feeling childish and incompetent.

What I should do is call one of the officers back at the station, but they all hated my guts and didn't trust me…

I stared at the suitcase on the floor. Nova had time to hang up new clothes, but didn't unload the suitcase, I noted. It was one more minor detail that made me think something was off…

Nova chewed on her bottom lip and it looked like she was fighting back tears. "I don't know. Maybe M-Martin picked the lock. He c-can be pretty clever when he w-wants to be."

"Do me a favor. Call him now, and I'll go take a look outside. Okay?"

Nova gave me a nervous nod, then opened one of the kitchen drawers. She took out a cheap flip phone and started dialing.

"He w-won't recognize this number. I left my cell behind when we m-moved. This was just a pr-prepaid ph-phone I p-picked up," she explained, pressing the phone to her ear.

Even though I'd said I was going outside to check, I stood still, watching her place the call. Please let the husband pick up the phone and say he has the girl, I hoped.

What if someone from Northfolk took this child? That thought made me queasy. The last thing I needed was another run-in with a bad dude in Northfolk. But if someone from here did this...then I had to do something to help this woman and her child.

Internally, I quivered at the thought. Why couldn't some other officer have taken this call? I wondered, exasperated.

"P-prick!" Nova snapped the phone back shut.

"You didn't leave a message," I pointed out.

"He never ch-checks his m-messages," Nova explained, placing the phone on the kitchen counter.

I took my own cell out, dialing the number I'd written down in my notebook. After three rings, the phone went to an automated voicemail box.

"Martin Nesbitt, this is Officer Ellie James with the Northfolk police department. I need to speak with you right away. It's urgent. Call me back at this number, please."

I started for the front door, eager to check outside, but then I stopped in the entranceway. I stared down at a pair of women's running shoes. They were muddy. "Your daughter's shoes. Where are they?"

Nova's eyes widened as her gaze followed mine. "Sh-she h-had sparkly orange sn-sneakers on when we got h-here yesterday." Her eyes went fuzzy, her lips curling with anger. "If she put her shoes on, then she must have gone with him w-willingly! But w-why would she do that?"

"Ma'am, I'm not sure. Hopefully, your husband will call back soon and clear this whole thing up. But for now, I'm going to check outside and then contact my sergeant about your daughter. Can you get some pictures together for me? If we issue an Amber Alert, I'll need the most up-to-date photo you got..."

But Nova was shaking her head back and forth, her skin turning paler by the minute. "I don't have one. N-not even one ph-photo…" she breathed.

"I know you guys just moved here, but how about a pic on your cell phone?"

But Nova kept shaking her head. "I can't believe it. I d-don't even have one picture of my little girl. How insane is th-that?" She looked spacey now, and once again, I wondered if she might be using drugs.

"Don't worry, ma'am. We'll get one. Maybe from a family member, or friend? Or if you could just pull up one of your albums on Facebook or Instagram…that will work, too."

"No," Nova said, firmly, her eyes zeroing in on mine.

"No?"

How could this woman not have any pictures of her own daughter? It seemed completely unfeasible, but if she really was afraid of her husband maybe she did leave everything behind…

"I wasn't allowed to have a Facebook profile. I-I don't even know what I-Instagram is, honestly. M-Martin was j-jealous. Controlling. He's d-dangerous, I told you…"

Yes. He was *dangerous*. That was about the only thing she'd made clear so far. I couldn't shake the feeling that there was something else—something she *wasn't* telling me.

"Family or friends with pictures…?"

"I don't really have any family. And any fr-friends I had…w-well, that was w-way before I married M-Martin."

Surely, she had pictures at her house in Tennessee, I considered. But Tennessee was a day's drive away, and I needed something now.

"What about pre-school or daycare? Any photos on file they could fax over to my office?"

Nova cleared her throat. "Lily isn't in pr-preschool yet. M-Martin wanted me to homeschool her. Can you believe that? Homeschool! M-Me! I don't even b-believe in that crap…" she snapped, looking angry again. Her arms hung loosely at her sides,

24

but she was shaking. As helpless as she seemed, I honestly felt the same.

"Keep trying to call him, okay? And this time leave a message," I urged, heading out to the front yard.

I walked around the front and back of the property. There was a backdrop of woods behind the house, but the trees were thin and sparse, so it was easy to see through the wooded space. I called out, "Lily!", but instantly felt silly as my own voice bounced back in my face.

It was eerily quiet out here. And as I walked around the entire house and yard space, I saw no signs of a child. My stomach churned. Something feels so wrong about this...

After going around three times and circling through the woods, I combed the ground in front of the house.

If Lily was hiding, she would surely have come out by now.

No pictures. Only new clothes and toys. It was like a child hadn't even been here, I thought, spinning around in circles. I closed my eyes and pictured my niece, Chelsea. Her room was like a landmine of toys, my sister's house a jungle gym of play-things. But Nova's house was scrubbed clean, not a toy or stray article of clothing in sight.

But she did say they just moved here, I reminded myself.

There was a blue Celica parked at the side of the house, which I assumed belonged to Nova. I peered in through the passenger window. There was no little girl hiding inside.

And no car seat in the vehicle either, I noted. How did she get Lily here without a car seat?

No toys or clutter in the backseat. Nothing. Almost like the child doesn't even exist, I thought, curiously.

My eyes floated across the field to the Appleton Farm. If I remembered correctly, Clara Appleton owned all this land. She was probably the one renting out the house to Nova.

Maybe the neighbor saw something...anything that could help me find this faceless child...

# CHAPTER THREE

*The Neighbor*

## CLARA

Cradling a cup of coffee in my hands, I watched Officer Ellie James through the dining room window as she stood in front of the cabin next door.

I heard Nova Nesbitt scream this morning. But still, I did nothing to help her.

My new tenant had sent me the first month's rent and a security deposit last month, and she had arrived just yesterday as planned. It was late when she got in, much too late in my opinion, but maybe she got lost or turned around on her drive into town.

I'd been tempted to go over and talk to her, to introduce myself, but I'd refrained. Landlords are known for being nosy. I didn't want to be like that. But it did feel strange having a neighbor again. With my oldest daughter in Texas, I'd grown accustomed to the quiet and lonesome life on the farm. Knowing that another human being was only a few strides away was a strange, yet welcome, feeling.

Last night, I'd watched the lights in the cabin pop off and on, wondering what Nova was up to. And then this morning, I'd been awake, toasting bread like I did every morning, when the jarring scream had ripped the air.

And now the police are here...

As the owner of the property, I probably should have gone over there and seen if something was wrong. That would have been the normal thing to do. Any sort of terrible thing could have happened related to the house—a fallen fan, a rusty nail...

But the last thing I wanted was contact with the police.

Hot coffee sloshed out the sides of my cup, dribbling between my fingers and down my arm. My mind drifted across the field to the old rickety barn at the back of the property. It used to house cattle and horses, back when Andy was here. But now it was empty. Well, except for one thing...

My hands shook uncontrollably until I lost my grip on the mug completely. It hit the floor with a dull thud just as I saw the young officer crossing the field straight toward my house. I wrung my now empty hands together, trying to steady the tremors.

The milky brown stain at my feet spread out like a halo around the unbroken mug. It reminded me of blood. Dark, thick, unrelenting blood...

Smoothing my favorite flannel shirt, I took a deep breath then went to the front door to meet her. Why does she want to talk to me?

I opened the door before she could knock, forcing a smile as I did. I recognized Officer Ellie James—she was the spitting image of her mother, Barbara. Barb and my late mother, Carol, used to hang around when they were younger. But I doubted that Officer James knew that fact or cared about it.

"How can I help you, officer?" I croaked, then grimaced at my own voice. After a decade of not smoking, I'd recently started up again. And it was obvious from the scratchy tone of my voice. I tried to swallow the lump that was forming in my throat, but it felt like a fishbone was lodged in my windpipe. Probably cancer from the cigarettes already, I lamented.

"You own the cabin next door, is that right, ma'am?"

Surprisingly, Officer James looked more nervous than I felt. She was young, and pretty, too, with a soft, freckled face. But she was wearing too much makeup, in my opinion, the lines of her eyeliner drawn out in a way that reminded me of an Egyptian princess.

"I do," I said, clearing my throat. "Everything alright over there?"

"When did Nova and Lily move in?" she asked, dodging my question.

"They came in late last night. From Tennessee. Quite a drive, you know? I was asleep. But I heard the car door, and I saw the lights go on over there."

"Did you see anything else? A child outside? Any other cars on the property?" Officer James held a small notebook in one hand, and with her other hand, she flicked her pen open and closed.

A sudden memory fluttered through my mind, then dissolved.

"Um, yeah, I did. Woke up around one in the morning, I guess it was. A second car was out there. Thought it might be her boyfriend, or someone helping her move. Not my business, you know? But I did think it was a little late for visitors..."

"What sort of make and model was this second car?" Officer James looked alert now, and she started writing something in that notebook of hers.

"I couldn't say. Too dark. Aren't any flood lights out there, you know? And the porch light wasn't on either. I heard the car pull in and the door slamming shut. Never saw a child. I guess it might have been a truck I saw..."

"Did you see anyone get out of this truck? This is important, ma'am."

I closed my eyes, thinking. "I only looked out there for a

second. Didn't want to look like a peeping tom. I think they were wearing a hood. Like a hoodie sweatshirt. And they were carrying something. Maybe she was carrying her daughter in her arms. Not sure though. Why? Something happened?"

"Your new tenant's daughter is missing. Please, if you see anything, or think of anything else, call me." She snapped her notebook shut then dug around for a business card. "Oh, and we may need to come back and search your property. All this land, if it comes down to it. Right now, we're still waiting to hear from the husband."

I tried to keep a straight face as I nodded obediently, but my throat felt like it was closing up completely. Despite feeling like I couldn't breathe, I was itching for a cigarette.

Officer James added, "Most likely, the husband took her. They recently split up. Divorces are so messy…" The young officer bit her lip, as though she'd said too much, then handed me a stiff business card.

"I will call you if I do. Thanks." I closed the door, letting out a long whoosh of breath.

I listened to the sound of the patrol car pulling out as I straightened up the kitchen. Cleaning was one thing I liked to do when I got nervous. Smoking was another.

Back in the kitchen, I gathered up the mug, discovering that a small chunk of ceramic had come loose. I threw it away, then went into my bedroom to search for some sort of carpet cleaner. Anything to take my mind off smoking, and the jarring police visit.

The stain would be hard to get out. Usually, I was careful, rarely needing cleaners to fix my mistakes.

I stopped for a moment to smooth out the edges of my bedspread, my fingers trembling. My pack of Camels was tucked away in my bedside drawer, within reach.

But instead, I picked up one of the stuffed bunnies my husband made for me, squeezing it tightly to my chest.

# CHAPTER FOUR

### *The Mother*

## NOVA

I guess it all started on the day I was born. *Choices. I tend to make the wrong ones.* Specifically, I've always been drawn to the wrong people, and it started with my mom and dad. Mama didn't want me. Even before she met me, she wanted to get rid of me. Somehow, my dad talked her into having me, but when she left the hospital after giving birth, she didn't take me with her.

I guess I should have been grateful toward him. If not for him, I'd be a goopy mass of medical waste. But truth was, he didn't really want me either. Sometimes, I wondered if I would have been better off if mama would have gone with her choice, instead of his.

A psychiatrist could psychoanalyze me pretty quickly—I was that cliched patient, the one who made it easy to set forth guidelines and criteria for dysfunction—mama left me, and daddy abused me, so I was destined to choose shitty partners as a result. Simple as that. My entire psychiatric profile wrapped up in a neat little bow.

But there weren't any warning signs when it came to Martin, not really. He was sweet, tender even, for those first two years we dated...but looking back, he wasn't the only bad choice I made. In high school, I chose the wrong friends. My dating life before Martin was a nightmare.

*How could I have chosen so wrongly? How could I have been so blind?*

Moonlight slithered through the open window above my bed. I had an upside-down view of the stars. There were so many of them, more stars than I'd ever seen from my window back home in Tennessee.

They made me feel insignificant. And that's exactly how I wanted to feel when I brought Lily to the cabin—like particles of dust in the wind, floating around unseen and unkept. *Forgotten.*

*Why couldn't Martin just forget us? Why couldn't he let us go?*

Back in Granton, our home was like a battleground. But I guess, for Martin, it wasn't so bad because he was the one waging war. I was just a casualty.

*And now Lily is a casualty too.*

I could still taste the bottle of wine I'd drank before bed. Turning on my side didn't help. I curled my knees to my chest, fighting back the urge to throw up.

It wasn't morning, but it wasn't night, I could tell from the slant of the moon. *It must be two, maybe three, in the morning now? Where is my daughter? Is she sleeping? Is she safe?*

My mouth watered with nausea as I fumbled around with the covers, searching for my cell phone in the dark. Instead I found my pack of Listerine strips. I slid one out and tossed it on the back of my tongue. I'd gotten into the habit of using them. Martin preferred fresh breath at all times.

I'd called Martin's phone nearly a hundred times today, asking him to call me back. Begging him to bring me my daughter. There was no point in keeping my location a secret anymore—he obvi-

31

ously already knew we were here. He'd taken my Lily. *Oh, god… Lily…*

I'd expected him to answer the phone, to demand that I come home if I ever wanted to see her again. But the calls went straight to voicemail.

*He's not going to give her back.*

I was too drunk to cry and too drunk to panic. My limbs felt numb and I hated myself for enjoying the nothingness I felt inside.

My entire *soul* was numb.

*I'm like a chunk of ice, pieces chipped away.*

*How much of me is left? Is there anything worth saving if I don't have Lily?*

*What if he took her and moved away, just like I tried to do? What if he decided that he didn't need me anymore? Now he can focus on Lily—a younger victim, a younger me…*

I couldn't hold it in anymore. I leapt from the bed and ran for the bathroom, barely reaching the commode before vomit sprang from my mouth and nose.

*What am I going to do? How will I get Lily back?*

I'd tried to reach that cop on her phone, but she hadn't been available.

*Dammit. I've lost Lily, and no one can help me save her. Not even the police.*

An Amber Alert wasn't issued. The cops wouldn't return my calls.

*What else can I do?*

Wiping the back of my mouth with my robe sleeve, I drifted down the hallway and back to my bedroom. Suddenly, I felt sober again. Dark shadows danced on the walls. I stared at one; it looked just like the dark silhouette of a man.

Panic slammed against my chest as I flipped on the bedroom light.

*Nothing. No one is in my room.*

I yanked the covers off the bed, my cell phone smacking the floor as it fell out of the crumpled blanket.

I stared at the screen, squinting sleep and drunkenness from my eyes, willing Martin to call me…to give her back…

I'd searched the woods and wandered around the property today, feeling helpless. But I couldn't look for long because every time I tried to go outside, invisible walls came crushing in and I couldn't breathe…

But hunger is a disgusting thing—after a while, it supersedes all rational thought. I'd barely eaten in two days, so I'd gone out to the supermarket at dusk. I'd ran up and down the aisles, like a madwoman, breathing in through my nose and out through my mouth, finally settling on some booze and peanut butter.

I thought that by the time the sun went down, Martin would call or show up.

But he never called. He never came.

*I couldn't protect Lily in Tennessee, and I can't protect her now.*

Martin wouldn't give her back unless he wanted to, and they were probably long gone by now.

*Maybe I'm like mama and I never should have had a kid in the first place. At least not until I had a partner better than Martin.*

The tiny black phone in my hand was foreign. My white iPhone I'd left behind was larger, and much more capable. I squinted down at the tiny screen. No missed calls, but there was one text message. My heart leapt as I clicked on it, praying it was from Martin.

My eyes stung with tears as I saw who it was from. *Al.*

**Al: You told me to wait at least 24 hours before texting you on this number. I hope you're okay…I've been so worried about you.**

I laid back down on the bed, clutching the phone like an old friend. A message from Al was like salve on an open wound. I typed out a message in response, then erased it.

*What if it's not really Al? What if it's Martin trying to trick me?*

Al and I had been talking for almost a year, but we hadn't communicated over text until now. Usually we just chatted online. But I'd confessed I was leaving Martin and had texted my new number. I'd warned Al not to message me on it until I was far away from Granton.

Martin frequently looked through my cell phone and checked my internet history. He checked my emails daily, too, although no one ever emailed me anymore.

Knitting was my one hobby he seemed to support—probably because his own mother used to knit—and he never minded when I looked up ideas or asked for advice in my knitting chat room. That's where I'd met Al. I didn't really care much for knitting, but it was the one place I had a friend.

And now, seeing a message from my friend on my cell phone, I was overcome with relief.

I typed out another message, clicking send before I could change my mind.

**Me: I don't know what to do. I'm so scared. He found out where I am. When I woke up this morning, Lily was gone. He took my bunny away.**

I stared at the phone, nibbling on a hangnail as I waited for a response. Al was the only person who knew my situation, who understood what this getaway meant for me and Lily.

Suddenly, the phone started ringing, the sound of it so shocking, so surreal. I saw Al's name flash up on the screen. After a year of only talking online, I was about to hear Al's voice.

I took a deep breath then answered. "I-Is that r-really you?"

# CHAPTER FIVE

*The Cop*

**ELLIE**

Barbara James was a worrier. Not only did she worry about me, but everything. I'd tried to stay quiet, sneaking around my bedroom like I was fifteen years old again, but it was only a matter of time before she realized I was still awake.

"Shit." I clenched my teeth as she rapped on my bedroom door. The light was off, but the computer was emitting a low stream of light that could be seen from under the door.

"Are you awake in there?" The knob rattled and groaned. And then, "Why did you lock your door?" Her voice was muffled on the other side.

She sounded hurt. The pang in her voice triggered a distant memory: the first time I'd lied to her. My best friend Priscilla and I had snuck bottles of cheap alcohol into my room after our seventh grade Valentine's dance. My mother suspected we were drinking, but I swore to her that we weren't. Only a few days later she found a bottle of Boone's Farm stuffed under my bed. *Why did you lie to me? Who are you, Ellie?* she'd asked. I'd never forgotten that look of disappointment on her face; it cut me to the core. But it wouldn't be the last time I disappointed my mother...

I got up and opened the door, half-expecting a younger version of her—soft brown curls around her face and smile lines sprouting from her nervous eyes...

But this older version was wearing a frilly button-down nightgown. Her now-thinning, now-white hair was in rollers, her face scrubbed and cleaned to perfection. She didn't look seventy, but the lines around her eyes had deepened and there were spidery crinkles around her mouth.

"I thought I heard typing in here," she said, making it sound like an accusation.

"Yes, mother. I'm *working*. Remember my job? When I agreed to keep living with you, I didn't agree to a curfew."

She smiled, but the smile didn't reach her eyes. "I know that, honey. I was just worried. Are you working on something important? I'm not very tired. Perhaps I could help..." She glanced over my shoulder, squinting at my desk screen even though I knew she couldn't read it from here without her glasses.

"No...you should get your rest."

"Oh, come on, Ellie. Your ol' mom loves a good mystery. I was a big fan of Nancy Drew when I was a girl. Now I can tell something's on your mind. You barely ate anything at dinner."

Too tired to put up a fight, I said, "Okay."

Talking through the case with someone else suddenly seemed like a good idea. I sat down in my computer chair and mom sat down on my bed. I scooted up closer to the screen, rubbing my sleep-filled eyes.

"Okay. There's this new woman in town, renting out the cabin on the Appleton Farm. She called us in this morning because apparently, her husband kidnapped his own daughter."

Mom's perfectly plucked eyebrows shot up. "Really? How old is the daughter?"

"Four. And that's what's bothering me. The mom says he's abusive and so she and the daughter ran away from him. But as soon as she got settled into her new place, he came and took her back."

"Well, maybe he just took her back home. That doesn't mean he hurt her. It sort of sounds like this woman is the one who ran off with her in the first place. Why not just divorce the man and do things properly?" Mom sniffed the air, looking around my room as though this case had become considerably less interesting.

But I knew that wasn't the real reason. My dad never beat up my mom, but he'd been verbally abusive toward her for as long as I could remember, up until the day he died. Although she was too proud to admit it, she knew a thing or two about dysfunctional marriages.

"Well, you're sort of right. I mean, she doesn't have a restraining order against the guy. They're not divorced yet. Technically, taking his daughter back isn't illegal."

"What did Sam say?"

It sounded strange, hearing her call my boss, Sergeant DelGrande, by his first name.

"That I should keep trying to reach the husband, then follow up with her again tomorrow. He said that these domestic squabbles usually blow over, and that next time I should suggest she get a lawyer and handle the custody dispute in court. It's not really a criminal matter unless we have reason to believe the child is in danger."

"What about his criminal record? Is he a dangerous guy?" Mom leaned forward, squinting at the computer again. A list of criminal cases lined my screen. I'd looked up all men in Tennessee with the last name 'Nesbitt'.

"Not on paper. He's had two traffic tickets. That's it. There's a couple other men on here with the same name, but they don't have the same birthday or identifying characteristics as the one who lives in Granton."

37

"So, he's not a criminal. That's a good sign. But that doesn't mean he's not guilty. Abuse can be so subtle...so well hidden sometimes." Mom shifted around on the bed, looking uncomfortable. In the green glow of the computer screen, she looked gaunt and ghoulish.

"I found something I could work with though. It's illegal to take your child away to another state without a court order. So, maybe I could nail him for that. Nova's in West Virginia and he's in Tennessee. If he grabbed the girl and crossed state lines..."

"Or you could nail *her*," Mom corrected me, fluffing her rollers.

"What do you mean?"

"Her home is in Tennessee, right? I bet it still says Tennessee on her driver's license. If she up and took the daughter away to West Virginia, then she's the one in trouble here. Have you even looked up her criminal record?"

Instantly, I felt like a moron. "No, I haven't. But you're right. I should. I've been looking up info on him for the past hour."

Determined now, I scooted my chair up closer and typed in 'Nova Nesbitt' in the search box. I widened my criteria, searching all states and genders.

Instantly, a list popped up and Nova's name was at the very top. I gasped as a row of charges loaded beneath her name.

*Domestic Battery.*

*Criminal Confinement.*

*Strangulation.*

"Holy shit."

I leaned back in my chair, full of disbelief. My mind floated back to the wispy, stuttering woman I met this morning. She seemed so fragile, so anxious. Could she be the real abuser in this situation? I wondered, incredulously. My gut was saying: no.

"Mom, you're the best. I was so focused on him and whether the child was in danger, that I never looked up more info on her. It sounds like there are some major issues going on in the family and I need to figure this out."

38

I expected my mom to make a crack about my investigative skills or get on me for cussing, but she just looked tired and worried. She patted me on the shoulder and stood up.

"Don't go out there by yourself. You know what happened last time…"

I stiffened. "What happened to Ezra Clark wasn't my fault. I was doing things by the book…"

"This is a small town, Ellie. And everyone in it knew Ezra was a mean drunk." My mother's back was to me, her hand resting on the doorknob in the dark.

So, even my mother thinks I'm a cop killer, I thought, squeezing the arms of my computer chair.

"Whether he was a drunk or a well-known cop, doesn't give him the right to hit his wife. And it certainly didn't give him the right to grab for my gun when I went to arrest him," I hissed, waiting for her to turn around.

"I know, honey. I know," she said, letting herself out and pulling the door closed behind her.

Turning back to the computer screen, I stared at the list of Nova's charges until the words turned blurry through my tears. Maybe she really was a criminal. A reckless woman who assaulted her husband and skipped town with their child…

Maybe she wasn't all that she seemed. Or…maybe she just got a bad rap like I did when I'd defended myself against Ezra Clark…

# CHAPTER SIX

## *The Neighbor*

### CLARA

I stopped sleeping after Krissy left. The house had gone quiet ever since she moved to Texas with her husband, Tim. Now twenty, she was no longer my little girl, but a woman on her own with her own family to take care of and worry about.

It had been two years since she left, but still, sometimes I thought I could hear her—the *tap tap tap* of her typing. That girl was always typing, either writing a story or doing research for some cause she wanted to fight for. And sometimes I heard the younger versions of her—Krissy with her Hot Wheels, the metal wheels scraping on the hardwood floors and running up the sides of the walls. It used to aggravate me to no end. I'd be reading a book or cooking supper, and here she'd come, buzzing down the hall with those obnoxious cars.

And Annie, too. Sometimes I still heard Annie. Unlike Krissy, Annie never aged—her sounds were always that of a three-year-old. Sucking on her bottle that I never got the chance to break her from. Giggling. Her laughter, a cute little snort. I'd open the bathroom door, expecting to find Annie in there taking a bubble bath, running little rubber duckies around the porcelain walls of the tub…

There were pieces of them all over the farm, like pieces of old ghosts. I couldn't sleep in my own bed because Andy would be there waiting. I could feel the pressure of his weight, lying on his side of the bed…

Lately, I'd taken to leaving the TV on. Twenty-four hours a day someone was talking—Ellen DeGeneres, Dr. Phil, Judge Judy…But tonight, I couldn't bear to listen. There was something about listening to other people's lives that I could no longer stand. It felt stupid, really, living vicariously through other people. Meanwhile, I was wasting away, turning into a ghost myself, here on the farm.

It was late, nearly three in the morning, and nothing good was ever on at this time. A pale sliver of light poked through the curtains and there was a tightening in my throat. I hadn't smoked in hours, but still, my mouth and throat felt dry.

Quietly, I tiptoed closer to the dining room window, peeking through the small gap in the curtains. Praying my new tenant wouldn't catch me spying on her again.

But there wasn't much to see, just a slippery shadow moving around behind the curtains in her bedroom window.

News of Nova's missing daughter hadn't made the nightly news. I'd seen her wandering the property in the middle of the day, but she hadn't been out there long. I was so worried she'd come to my door and knock, but she never did. She'd ran around, frantic-like, then ran back inside.

Suddenly, the back-porch light of the cabin popped on and off. Then on again. From across the field, I watched my tenant emerge through the back-screen door. She was bent at the waist, dragging something over the threshold and then, she pulled a large object across the ground.

In the dark, it looked like a long, black bag.

I couldn't see her face as she tugged and pulled, but her hair whipped around wildly in the wind until eventually, she disappeared through the trees at the back of the property.

# CHAPTER SEVEN

## *The Cop*

### ELLIE

Northfolk's police station was a small brick building, reminiscent of a 1940s school house. On a Sunday morning, there was no one manning the front desk, the entire building deserted. I let myself in, using my key, then flipped on lights as I juggled my coffee and purse.

Working on Sundays wasn't typical for me. Usually, there was no reason to. The four other officers and I rotated the on-call cell phone every weekend, and responded to emergencies as needed, calling for back-up when necessary.

But rarely did the phone ever ring.

This was Roland's weekend, but I didn't expect to see him either. He didn't come in on weekends; sometimes he didn't even work on *weekdays*.

The hallway was cold and colorless, one smoky lightbulb flickering in and out. I used another key to let myself into my office, then frowned at my neatly arranged desk. In the movies, police officers always had messy desks because they were too busy out in the field to deal with paperwork. But most days, I had more than enough time to finish my work and clean my office, too.

The organization in my office felt like a niggling sign of failure.

I took a seat behind the desk and fired up my computer. At home, my searches were more limited. I needed to know more about Nova Nesbitt. Needed to see that police report from when she was charged with all those awful crimes.

The computer was taking forever to load, probably installing some useless update. That's when I heard the front door to the building click open and shut. Hadn't I locked it behind me?

"Yooo-hooo!" a man's voice bellowed. *Roland.* He'd probably seen my cruiser parked out front and decided to stop in just because. I released an internal groan.

Roland was nearly forty, and balding, but still acted like a frat boy, always telling inappropriate jokes and flirting with the women he was supposed to be protecting.

"What's up, Sharp?" *Sharp* was short for *Sharp Shooter*, another stupid nickname because I wasn't as experienced or interested in guns as some of my male compatriots. And also, a more sinister reference…they still looked at me as *that* cop, the one who had shot a fellow officer. A *superior* officer, to make matters worse.

It didn't matter that the shooting was justified…no one seemed to care about the actual details of what happened that day with Ezra Clark's death…they simply wanted to blame the newbie that had killed a veteran officer.

When they looked at me, I could see it in their eyes…*She killed a cop. She killed one of us. She can't be trusted.*

But I did the right thing, didn't I? Sometimes they made me doubt myself…and plans to join a big city force had dissipated. If I couldn't make it in this small town, I couldn't make it anywhere…

Roland's head popped through my door, his smile wolfish and mean. "Whatcha doing here on a Sunday, huh? Looking up online pointers for your shooting exam?" He chuckled at his own joke, hard enough that his laughs evaporated into wheezy coughs.

I was seized by the sudden desire to stand up and punch him.

"Working on a case," I grumbled, shifting unimportant papers around on my desk. He made me uncomfortable and for a brief moment, as he stood in the doorway surveying me, I forgot why I'd come in in the first place. "What can I do for you, Roland?" I sighed.

"Saw your car. And that reminded me. There were a few messages for ya, on Saturday. From some girl."

I gripped the edge of my desk with both hands. "Why didn't you call my personal cell? By girl, do you mean a woman? Was it Nova Nesbitt?"

"Well, I didn't get the messages until this morning. But yeah, I think that's the name she said in her message."

"Roland! You're *on-call*. That means you have to answer the phone when it rings. How hard is that to understand? What if it was an emergency?"

Roland shrugged, that lopsided smile coming back. "So, shoot me. It was an honest mistake." His face flickered with anger on the word *shoot*.

His eyes were red-rimmed and glassy. He'd probably been down at Mick's Lounge when the calls came in. Roland and some of the other guys spent their free time at Mick's, or Prissy's, the strip club on I-90. Sometimes they spent their on-the-clock hours there too. They weren't all bad guys, but Roland was definitely the worst in the group. *He's the reason some male cops get bad raps*, I thought, shaking my head.

In a town where there were more bars than restaurants, and the closest thing to a strip mall was a strip club with a Dollar Tree attached, what could I really expect? Twenty-five years ago, Roland was playing football, or some other meathead sport that made him look cool, while I was being ignored and/or teased by guys just like him. Now he was just an older, fatter version of himself, but he had the power and authority that came with being a cop.

"Welp, if it was an emergency, she should have called 911. Anyway, she mentioned your name in the message, so I thought I'd pass it along. Something about a dispute with the husband and kid? Sounds like a domestic dispute that the courts should be handling…"

My jaw clenched. It was a terrible habit that often resulted in midnight migraines.

I clicked my computer screen off and gathered up my bag and keys, then I locked the door to my office behind me, nudging him aside with my purse.

I was going to walk out, but then I changed my mind. Turning around, I narrowed my eyes at Roland.

"You know what? I'll take that on-call cell phone," I snapped.

Another shrug. "Hey, that works for me." He took the cell phone out of his back pocket and held it over my head, just out of reach. *You must be fucking kidding me.* I was far from petite, but I hadn't grown an inch since middle school. Roland's six-foot frame towered over my five-foot two-inches.

My fist struck the center of his abdomen and he let out a groan. Bent at the waist, I grabbed the cell phone as it clattered on the floor by my feet.

Roland looked up at me, smiling as he clutched his waistline. His cheeks were the color of cherry blossoms. "You got a thing for picking on other officers, don't you? Maybe I should report you to the sarge for assault…"

"Go right ahead."

Unlike some of the guys, Sergeant DelGrande was more supportive of me.

Moments later, I roared out of the parking lot, cussing myself for letting Roland get to me…and for not writing my personal cell number on the back of the business card I gave to Nova. The card had my office extension on it and the on-call number. But

46

if she'd tried my office yesterday, then it would have just rung and rung, eventually going straight to voicemail.

Wildly, I drove around the twisty inclines of the Appalachians, afraid of what I might find. What if Nova found her daughter on the property and I wasn't there to help? Images of bloody, bloated toddlers sliced through my head like razors. What if her husband showed up and tried to hurt her? I clenched my teeth together so hard I could almost hear the enamel cracking.

Someone should have been there to take her call, dammit!

Despite the beauty of the rugged, flat-topped highlands and majestic mountain ridges that seemed to reach the sun, the town itself looked like an ashtray. Like there was some sort of smoking giant, flicking its filth all over the city, and onto the people who lived here.

The houses were taped together, some barely standing. Boarded up windows and sagging roofs. Windows plastered shut with cardboard or old blankets. And the rivers and creeks were so full of garbage you couldn't swim or fish. It seemed so wrong to see so much poverty amongst such a beautiful backdrop, but this town *was* poor. Most of its income came from tourism in the summer and springtime, thanks to hikers and ATV enthusiasts.

I couldn't breathe when I pulled up in front of the house. Please let Nova be okay…I can't afford to make another mistake that keeps me ostracized even more by my peers…

The cabin was quiet and dark, and there was something *off* about the place as soon as I put my cruiser in park.

I approached the cabin, taking in more details than I had on my first visit.

The grass was a soupy wasteland after last night's rain and mosquitoes buzzed around my pant legs as I made my way up to the door.

I could still see Nova, the way she'd looked two days ago, desperation in her eyes as she ran out to meet me in her robe.

She'd been so scared…but I didn't know what to do for her then. And I still didn't, I realized.

I knocked softly at first. But then, when no one came to answer, I gave the door a hard, authoritative rap. Her Celica was parked in the same spot it had been the night before.

There were two windows on either side of the front door. I tried to peek through both, eager to spot some sort of movement through the off-white curtains. Nothing. A sick feeling rose in my stomach.

Slowly, I moved around the right side of the house, looking in side windows and peeking in the car as I passed it.

Maybe Nova was still asleep? After all, it was Sunday. Most people, besides church-goers like my mom and her parish, liked to sleep in on the weekends. I silently prayed that that was the case with Nova.

As I reached the backside of the cabin, I immediately noticed that the back door was ajar. A tiny sliver of light peeped out through the crack.

I knocked harder, jarring the door, and I willed myself to be patient. I'd never barged into anyone's house before, and I didn't want to start now. Without a warrant, I had no business letting myself inside.

But if something horrible had happened to her…if that *dangerous* husband of hers had showed up…then it was on me for not taking her more seriously.

"Nova?" I shout-whispered through the crack.

I put my hand on the knob and nudged the door open a few more centimeters. "It's Officer Ellie James. I need to follow up with you."

There were no sounds of movement inside and I couldn't see anything through the crack besides the tiny bit of light coming from the kitchen.

"I'm coming in, ma'am," I warned. The proper protocol would be to call for some sort of back-up, or at the very least, take out my firearm. But the last thing I wanted was to call the very colleagues who didn't trust me, and probably wouldn't have my back anyway.

"Damn you, Nova," I mumbled, stepping back from the door. Clumsily, I unholstered my pistol and flipped the safety off. I gripped it in my right hand, praying I wouldn't need to use it ever again…

"Nova, I'm coming in now." I kicked the door and was instantly met with some sort of resistance.

"What the hell?" I nudged it again with my foot, grunting against whatever weight was pushed up behind it. There was something heavy laying on the other side of the door.

I couldn't get in the house without squeezing through the crack, and I wasn't sure what—or *who*—was behind the door. I took a deep breath and pushed my face up against the crack, trying to see what was jamming up the entranceway.

Instantly, I recognized the black duffel bag. It was the same one I'd seen laying in the middle of the kitchen floor the first time I'd met with Nova. But why was it so heavy? It was almost like it was filled with stones.

Using both hands, including the one with the gun, I gave the door another hard shove. The bag scooted forward a few inches, just enough for me to slip inside the cabin.

I called out for her three more times, then entered the kitchen. Glancing down at the bag, I saw that it was open and filled with hard, fist-sized rocks. Tentatively, I bent down to get a closer look. The rocks were smooth and all the same size.

Next to the rocks were three cylindrical containers with metal latches on top. They were empty but had some scummy red marks around the lids. What the hell?

I gripped the gun in both hands now, my voice shaky as I called out again, "It's Officer Ellie James, and I'm coming in." How many times am I going to say that? I wondered, clenching and unclenching my jaw. As I scooted, little by little, across the kitchen floor, the hairs on the back of my neck stood on end. Something was seriously wrong here, I could feel it in my bones…

It only took a few more seconds to find out what it was. I gasped as I entered the living room, instantly lowering my gun. A puddle of blood, wide as a coy pond, and so red it was almost purple, spread out from the center of the floor. My body swayed and shook as I stared at tiny white fragments at my feet. Kneeling for a closer look, I discovered the fragments were bone. Not just bone—they looked like human teeth.

# CHAPTER EIGHT

*The Neighbor*

## CLARA

In a perfect world, the FBI would have showed up at my rental property. But the blood had gone dry by the time two experts showed up to process the scene, and let's face it: the FBI doesn't give a damn about people in Northfolk.

I waited outside next to Officer James' police car, smoking a Camel. I'd gone all night without a cigarette, but this incident gave me the perfect excuse to fire one up. Smoke filled my lungs, sending little shocks of warmth to my head and my toes.

Officer Ellie James had asked me to stay. After all, I owned the cabin that was now the scene of a crime.

Leaning against the hood of my tenant's car, I puffed while watching the chaos around me unfold.

Two policemen I recognized, Roland Anderson and Michael Boyd, were standing less than two feet away, looking at something on one of their cell phones. Hard workers, those two, I thought, rolling my eyes.

The Sergeant was there too. I knew Sam DelGrande well. He

and Andy used to go fishing together sometimes. The sergeant and Officer James stood near the back of the cabin, chatting with one of the forensic guys, who was wearing a white, space-like suit.

The astronaut lookalike turned around and went back inside the cabin, and then Officer James and Sam came walking toward me. Damn. I don't want to deal with police, I thought, reluctantly stubbing out my cig on the ground beside me. Now that the cancer stick was gone, the lump was back. I swallowed it down and cleared my throat.

I didn't see the blood pool inside, but Officer James told me there was reason to believe that my new tenant or her child had been victims of foul play. *How much blood is there?* I'd asked her, horrified when she came to my door. *A lot*, that was all she said, over and over. Maybe it was just me, but Officer James looked stricken with fear, her face pale as the moon on a cold winter's night.

I'd been relatively calm. I'd even offered to make coffee for everyone. But Officer James had been insistent that I stay put. I couldn't help feeling like a suspect at this point, just standing around.

"Hi, Ms. Appleton. This is Sergeant DelGrande. I'd like you to repeat what you told me, please," Officer James said. Her face was tight and strained, her right cheek bulging in and out as she mashed her teeth together. Nervous like her mother, Barb, I realized.

Sam was old enough to be my father, but I considered him a friend. He was one of the few people in this town who remembered the farm when it was up and running.

Sam smiled and said, "Clara and I know each other, Ellie. How's Andy doing? I sure do miss the guy." Wrinkles branched out from the corners of his mouth and his once jet-black hair was stippled with silver now. He was a quiet man, but he had this seriousness about him that always commanded attention.

"I don't know. You'd have to ask his mistress, you know? Last I heard they were renting out a house on the beach. That damn fool can't even swim," I told him.

"I'm sorry to hear that, Clara." Sam's eyes softened.

Officer James' eyes flicked back and forth between us, then she nodded for me to tell him what I'd already told her twice.

Closing my eyes, I tried to recall the exact details again.

"I was up late watching the telly. Don't sleep well, never have. I saw a light come on from across the field right around three in the morning. Now I'm not usually a nosy person, you know? But I haven't had a tenant over here in years, so at first, that light startled me a bit." My cheeks flushed crimson. For some reason, it was more nerve-racking re-telling this to Sergeant Sam.

"What did you see?" Sam's eyes were narrowed, his face grim.

"Nothing, honest. There was a light on in the room that she was probably using as a bedroom. I heard about the ex-husband taking the girl, so I wondered what she was up to. I went to the window and looked out. And that's when—"

Sam's face leaned in closer to mine, expectantly. I could smell his aftershave and the faint hint of last night's Scotch on his breath. Andy was a Scotch man, too. I wondered if all those years ago, they weren't out fishing but instead were tying a few off at the bar...

"That's it. That's all I saw." My fingers itched, aware of the pack of smokes in my front jeans pocket. Could they tell I was holding back? Truth was, I just wanted them off my property.

"When did the light go off in her bedroom?" Sam asked, his face crumpled with disappointment that that was all I saw.

"Not sure. Stood there at the window, watching for a few minutes, and then I went to bed. It wasn't until around five or so, that I heard the truck pull in."

"What truck? Did you see what color it was?"

"Nah, it was still dark, and I was half asleep. I sleep on the couch now, ever since Andy moved out, and it was the headlights

53

casting shadows on the wall that stirred me. I got up, thinking about the child again, and I squinted through the same window. The truck parked behind the Celica. Might have been the same one I saw when they were moving in…and I heard the truck door open and close. I tried to get a look—I assumed it was the husband, you know? But I couldn't see a darn thing."

"Did she let him inside? Did you hear them fighting?" These questions came from Officer James now. She'd already asked them earlier.

"She must have cause the truck stayed put. Stood at the window for at least a half hour, waiting to see if I'd hear them fighting. Wondered if I might have to call the cops. I hate to say this, but I was a little worried about property damage, you know? On second thought, I probably should have gone and called the police anyway…I could have stopped him, or whoever it was, from hurting them." I held my hand up to my mouth in horror, then turned my face away so they couldn't see my tears.

"This is not your fault, Clara. Not your fault at all." Sam rested his hand on my shoulder.

"Did you see what time the truck left? Did you hear anything else, anything at all?" Officer James kept pushing.

I shook my head, wrestling with the tears. "I never heard a thing after that. Never saw anything either. My eyes got heavy… so I just laid back down on the couch, and next time I woke up was when Officer James was banging at my front door."

"Thank you. You can go on home now. We'll finish up here and then let you know when the cabin is safe to enter again. Promise me you won't go near it until it's been cleared?" Sam squeezed my shoulder and again, I thought about my husband, Andy.

"Oh, of course not. Wouldn't want to interfere. I just wish… will you let me know if there's anything else I can do?"

"Will do. But in the meantime, we have more officers and help on the way. We're going to comb this entire property and the woods," Officer James said, giving me a soft, worried smile. I could tell she was shaken from the incident, too. When she turned up at my door this morning, her eyes had looked wild and strange.

I thanked the officers again, then cast one last look at the cabin that had been in my family for years. It used to be a place for housing staff, migrant workers who helped on the farm and such, when it was large and thriving. When my mom was sick but didn't want to live with us, she stayed here until it was time for her to move into a nursing home. The cabin had always held good memories for me, even though it was a little dreary and run down. Now that had all changed.

Now it would be known as the place where a murder occurred.

# CHAPTER NINE

*The Cop*

**ELLIE**

Rainy weather arrived in earnest as the entire Northfolk police department and a handful of the sergeant's close family and friends searched the Appleton rental property and farm. We spread out like a fan, searching the woods and adjacent barn and outbuildings on Clara's side of the land.

Sergeant DelGrande took charge, instructing officers and especially volunteers not to touch anything.

"So, what do you think, huh? You think it's the kid's blood or hers in there?" Roland asked, nudging an old stump onto its side with his combat boot. I watched a treasure trove of pill bugs wriggle out from the underbelly. We used to call them roly-polies when I was a kid, I remembered.

"Fuck off, Roland. This is your fault." I kicked the log back over.

I walked off from him, focusing on the forest floor as I went. My eyes attempted to scan every square inch of it...but I was making myself dizzy and seeing red because I was so angry. I was

56

angry with Roland for not taking Nova Nesbitt's call. But I was angrier with myself—I'd been so scared about having another "incident" involving a domestic squabble that I'd treated Nova unfairly. She said her husband was dangerous—how many times had she made that clear? Could I have stopped this...? That question kept haunting me...

Pressing my back against the closest tree, I took a deep breath and tried to re-focus. A slow steady drizzle of rain trickled down through the trees. Surprisingly, it felt good as it touched my skin. I felt hot. *Rageful.* And one of my back molars felt chipped, from all the jaw flexing I'd been doing these past two days.

How could Roland be this stupid? Why hadn't he answered the call? And why hadn't I done more—if I trusted my colleagues more, maybe I would have asked a couple of the guys to provide security for Nova... I wondered, ruefully.

"Look, I'm sorry." Roland was back. He stooped down in front of me, placing his hands on my shoulders. He was close, too close, and I could smell his sweat and bitter cologne.

"Sorry, yeah? Well, you'll be sorry when Sarge finds out you didn't take the call. She was in trouble. She needed us, and now she's probably dead." I blinked back tears, trying to shake off the urge to cry. Roland was the last person I wanted to be vulnerable in front of...

Someone cleared their throat behind us. It was one of the forensics guys, Chad, I think he said his name was.

"Whoever that blood belongs to...they're probably dead. No one could sustain that much blood loss." His voice was soft but squeaky, and he looked apologetic as he shared this news.

My eyes darted around the woods, at the floating bodies combing through the trees and field. "She has to be here then. She couldn't have got far, not after losing that much blood..."

"Unless someone took her body with them," Roland said. He was chewing on a hang nail and staring off into space, like he didn't care as much as he should have.

"There's no evidence that someone dragged a body through that house, though," I said. "It's almost like she bled out in that one spot, then just evaporated."

"Want to come in with me? Take a look? I have a couple things I want to show you inside." Chad said.

For a second, Roland looked offended that he was directing the question to me and not him. "Keep searching," I told him, before following Chad back inside the dreaded cabin.

The last thing I wanted to do was look at, or smell, that blood again...but I owed this much to Nova. I should have listened to her...I should have trusted her the first time. I should have called in a sketch artist and tried to talk the sergeant into issuing an Amber Alert without the photo...should have given Nova some sort of police protection out here...should have done something more...*Shouldawouldacoulda.*

My face sagged as I stared at the rusty stain on the floor again. Whose blood was it? What sort of struggle had happened here...?

Another forensic tech was squatting down on his haunches, his back turned to me. "This." He held up a paper envelope in his gloved hand.

"What is it?"

"We collected three teeth. Two canines. One molar. Right now, we don't know who they came from, but I can say this: these teeth didn't fall out on their own. Whoever they belong to, they took a few blows to the face, at least."

"How can you tell?" I asked, shuddering in spite of myself. The throb in my own tooth pulsated relentlessly.

"Well, every tooth has its own characteristics. And no two oral cavities are alike. These teeth aren't complete, there's pieces missing from each one, which tells me that she suffered some sort of trauma, most likely some blows to the face."

"You said *she.* You definitely think it's Nova Nesbitt then? Could these possibly belong to a child?"

He shook his head. "Only dental records or DNA can tell us

for sure. But I'm certain these teeth belong to an adult female. You see, the upper and lower canines in men have this ridge that is more pronounced and frequently…"

But I was no longer listening. I turned on my heels and ran outside, shouting for Sergeant DelGrande. If Nova Nesbitt had been killed or assaulted here, then where was Lily? If the husband had killed Nova, then he'd most likely taken the child with him… This time, I couldn't hesitate. I needed to act and act fast.

***

"It doesn't make sense. Why don't they send one of the other guys? Why does it have to be you?"

I was shoving socks and underwear into my bag, while mom tried to talk me out of going to Granton, Tennessee.

"Why not me?" I said, standing up and stretching my neck side to side. My head and jaw were pounding so hard I couldn't think.

"It just seems like it would be more of a risk. I'm scared for you, honey," she croaked.

"Why? Because I don't have a penis, mom? I've mucked this up once, won't do it again. For all I know, that little girl could already be dead. And instead of trying to find her and hunt down Martin Nesbitt, I'm standing here, trying to convince my mom that it's the twenty-first century and women can do the same things as men."

I zipped my overnight bag closed and looked around my bedroom. Where did I put my keys?

"Look, you're right. I'm sorry. But it's an entire day's drive to Tennessee. Do you really have to leave tonight?"

"It's eight hours if I hurry. If I leave now, I'll make it by midnight."

My mom looked as though she might cry. But finally, she sighed and walked out of my room, leaving me to pack. My keys were on the floor next to my computer chair. I scooped them up and grabbed my bag, just as mom popped her head back in. She looked considerably less worried now.

"Roland and Mike just pulled in. They're going with you, they said."

"Oh, for fuck's sake." I tossed the bag over my right shoulder and kissed my mom on the cheek. "Call you when we get in," I promised.

# CHAPTER TEN

*The Neighbor*

## CLARA

Just like that, my new neighbor was gone. The cabin deserted. From across the field, it looked like a living, breathing, monster. The windows were two black holes for eyes, the door a gaping slash for a mouth.

They didn't find her body, or any other clues outside the cabin, as far as I knew. The last of the crew finished up at ten o'clock. I expected them to offer me some sort of protection, maybe a guard to watch over the place…but they didn't. They'd left me here alone, with my thoughts and my ghosts, and for some reason, that felt comforting. All the chaos and noise and company had made me a nervous wreck today.

Sam warned me not to disturb the scene, but I had to see it again. I just had to. It was my cabin, after all.

I let myself in the back door with my master key. I'd never felt like a criminal entering my own property before, but I did now. Could they arrest someone for disturbing a crime scene? Probably, I decided.

The kitchen was pitch black and dank. I stumbled over something in the middle of the floor, letting out a panicked cry. Even though I'd been determined not to turn on any lights, in case someone came back and saw me in here, I ran for the closest light switch. My fingers found the switch with practiced ease, and I let out a sigh of relief as the lights clicked on. There was a duffel bag in the middle of the kitchen floor. I stared at it, wondering what in the hell it was doing there.

I crept forward, confused by what my eyes were seeing. The bag was full of gray colored stones, like huge chunky bits of gravel but smooth in texture.

And the cannisters...Why would Nova put these here?

I didn't dare touch the bag, or anything else, for fear of leaving fingerprints. Of course, my own prints would be all over this place. I'd wiped it down and checked things thoroughly before I let my tenant move in. But still. I didn't want to disturb anything else.

Turning the kitchen light back off, I tiptoed into the living room. A dark brown stain covered the center of the floor. It looked dark, almost black.

I didn't dare move any closer to the blood stain. Instead I walked down the long dark hallway, holding my breath as I approached the two bedrooms at the end of the hall. My mind played tricks on me as I entered the master bedroom. Shadows swirled, and I fought the urge to turn on the lights again. Taking out my cell phone, I used the flashlight to look around Nova's room. The bed was unmade. A silky pink robe and panties lay crumpled up on the floor.

There was a strange smell in the air. Not blood or death, some sort of fruity perfume. Like coconut and cinnamon. Like Nova had been here only moments earlier...

Lily's room was empty and dark, the bed neatly made. It didn't even look like a child had slept here. My throat constricted as I rushed to get back outside. I burst through the back door, sucking in deep, wet breaths of cool night air.

The rain had started up again. It hadn't reached me yet, but I could hear it pinging on the leaves in the forest, moving closer and closer...I crossed the field, but instead of heading back into my house, I went to the barn.

It'd been empty for years, but still, I could smell horses and hay. Could see myself feeding the animals. Could see the way Andy used to dote on them. He'd rub the horses bare-handed till his hands went raw, cooing to them like tiny children. Sometimes I thought that man treated his animals better than his own family.

On the second tier was a hayloft. Blinking back tears, I tried not to think about all the days I hid up there as a child, drawing and writing while my grandpa performed his daily duties. He would pretend not to see me, although I'm certain he always knew...

The only thing left behind as a memory of my family's farm— the family before I had my own—was an ancient tractor that had belonged to my great-grandfather, Jack. Police looked in the barn today, but they didn't move the tractor. It was at least 150 years old, ancient and peeling, and obviously, hadn't been moved in years.

I laid down on my stomach, ignoring the dust and debris that coated my sweatshirt and jeans as I shimmied beneath the tractor. Luckily, I was still thin enough to slide underneath.

The false door wasn't visible to the naked eye—it just looked like part of the floor. But I knew which tiny crack I had to pry in order to get it open. I pulled it up just far enough to squirm inside.

Rung by rung, I descended a rickety, wooden ladder, praying I wouldn't catch any splinters along the way.

At the bottom was a small eight by eight room, previously used to store canned goods and supplies for the winter. Rows of metal shelving lined each side of the dank, dusty room. There was nothing down here anymore.

Nothing except for Andy.

He lay on his back, sleeping peacefully. Only he wasn't sleeping. And his face didn't look peaceful at all.

"Bastard," I huffed, staring at the man I used to love. His flesh was already rotting, falling away from the bones, and he smelled worse than a broken sewer line.

"Why did you have to come here? You screwed everything up!" My heart slammed in my chest as I hurried back up the ladder.

# CHAPTER ELEVEN

*The Cop*

**ELLIE**

Traffic was light and there were less cars on the road than I was used to on my daily morning drives to work in Northfolk. The air in Granton felt different. Thicker and foggy, and probably less clean, but it felt like there was more oxygen to go around for everyone.

Roland and Mike were nodding off in the backseat as I pulled into the Holiday Inn parking lot in Granton. I'd driven straight through, ignoring the urge to pee, because Roland had teased that I would have to stop first.

"Here we are," I grumbled, my pelvis achy as I put the car in park. Roland had called ahead and made the reservation. Personally, I didn't understand why we needed to sleep before confronting Martin Nesbitt. Every second that passed was a second too long. A second that Lily could be in danger.

"What time is it?" Mike stuck his head between the seats, squinting up at the neon glow of the hotel sign. The parking lot was empty, save for two cars, and one of them had to belong to staff because it had a Holiday Inn logo splashed along the side panel.

"One o'clock in the morning," I yawned. Mike was in his late twenties like me. He wasn't as big of a douchebag as Roland, but they were friends, and like the other guys, he didn't seem to trust me much since the shooting incident. In another life, maybe we could have been partners...friends...

Mike was wearing a tight black police top and jeans, his sandy blond hair poking out in sleepy little tufts on his head.

Roland groaned. "Bumpy ride. You should have let me drive," he glowered at me in the rearview mirror. Before leaving Northfolk, we'd squabbled over the keys and I'd won.

When I was fifteen, I'd got in a car with one of my older friends who'd had a few drinks too many and had pulled out in front of a Dodge Caravan before looking left at a stop sign. My seatbelt had saved my life, and hers too, but ever since that wreck, I liked being the one behind the wheel. I liked having my fate in my own hands whenever possible.

"I know sarge told us to crash for the night, then go see the husband in the morning. But I was thinking, why not go there now? It's only a couple miles away from here. Maybe we'll catch him off guard," I spoke softly, praying they'd both agree.

"Catching a man off guard, you say? Didn't you learn your lesson on that last time?" Roland sneered.

I gritted my teeth, fuming. Before I could defend myself on the Clark shooting for the hundredth time, Mike said, "Ease up, Roland. Guys, we just need to follow sarge's orders. He told us to go in the morning."

Roland pulled on the door handle from the backseat, but it was locked. Less than an hour into the drive, he'd asked me to stop at a Liquor Barn. *Tennessee doesn't sell alcohol after eleven. I don't want to miss my window*, he'd explained. Honestly, I was surprised he hadn't popped the top on a beer and drunk it in the backseat on the ride over.

A sudden urge to leave him locked in his hotel room and drive on to the Nesbitts', surged through me. I flexed my jaw, watching him struggle with the door handle in my rearview mirror.

"Unlock my door, Sharp. Mike, help her with the controls up there."

"I know how to unlock it," I snapped. I clicked a button and Roland jumped out.

"Sorry. I know he's an ass," Mike said, smiling weakly. Then he slid across the seat and followed him.

Frustrated, I gathered my purse and keys, then popped the trunk to get my bag. Just as I was taking it out, the on-call cell phone whirred in my pocket. I'd almost forgotten I had it on me, I'd been so focused on getting here and confronting Nova's husband.

It was a text message from an unknown number.

**Officer James, it's Chad Burch from forensics. I know it's late. I didn't want to wake you up, but can you call me first thing in the morning? I have some details to discuss with you about what I found out today, in regards to the Nesbitt case.**

I carried my bag in the crook of my arm, my mind racing as I wondered what Chad knew so far. Eager to get checked in so I could call him back, I hurried through the glass double doors and entered the lobby. Roland and Mike were nowhere to be found.

A young girl with cherry red hair and glittery green mascara was working the desk. She blushed when she saw me, and I had no doubt that Roland had just been flirting with her.

"They left you your room key," she said, giving me a timid smile as she slipped a plastic key card across the desk.

"Thank you. Let me know if they bother you," I said, cheeks flaming.

My room was on the second floor. I wasn't sure where Mike and Roland's rooms were, but I hoped they were far away.

Preferably on another floor completely. I tossed my bag on the queen-sized bed and turned on the lamp beside a small, wood-stained desk.

I sat down in a flimsy desk chair and kicked my shoes off while I waited for Chad to answer the phone. Please pick up, I silently chanted.

"Hey. I thought you might be asleep."

Relieved, I said, "What'd ya find? Did ya tell my sergeant?"

"I did. But I know you're the one who's been working the case from the start, so he said it was okay to call you directly." Chad cleared his throat and I thought I could hear him shuffling papers.

"Thank you, I appreciate that. I'm surprised you have something for me so fast."

"Well, me too, but this wasn't hard to figure out. The blood that we collected from the scene? You ready?"

My heart leapt into my throat. *What if the blood belongs to Lily?*

"The blood didn't come from a human. It's bovine. But there is some human blood embedded in the teeth."

*Bovine.* The term was familiar, but my heart was throbbing in my ears and I couldn't get my thoughts straight. "Wait. You mean cow's blood? Holy shit. Why would there be cow's blood in that cabin?"

"No clue. Could this be some sort of sacrificial killing? Was Nova into the occult, or anything like that?"

I stared at my overnight bag on the bed. "I have no idea what she was into. But there was a duffel bag full of rocks at the scene. Does that mean anything to you?"

The line was silent for several seconds. "No, it doesn't. But I just remembered something else. We found a cross in her garbage can in the kitchen. Animal blood, weird stones, and a cross. What's that make you think of?"

"Something satanic or ritualistic. But that seems a little far-fetched, don't ya think?" I pondered.

"Remember all those satanic ritual abuse cases in the eighties? They spread like wildfire but turned out to be untrue," Chad said.

"Yeah, I think I do…"

Chad coughed loudly, and I pulled my ear away from the phone. He came back on the line and said, "But, there's still the fact that there were human teeth. I mean, no one would be able to differentiate between mammal blood and human blood, not with the naked eye. But the ABC and Rh blood groups for the samples were different, so I automatically knew it wasn't human. But from a cow…wow, I've never seen that happen before. Are there farm animals in that barn next door?"

"No. There used to be, I think, but not for years."

A sudden thought was taking shape in my mind. What if Martin Nesbitt wanted us to think his wife and child were dead? What if he kidnapped the daughter, then came back for the wife… maybe Lily's still alive, I considered. Maybe the cow's blood was a decoy…?

"Is that it, Chad?" I asked, shoving my feet back into my shoes and standing up.

"If you can get dental records for Nova and a DNA sample, either from a close relative or from a toothbrush, or something at her house, that would help immensely. Her fingerprints are already on file because she's been in the system before."

"Okay. Thanks, Chad." I snapped the phone shut and grabbed my keys. I couldn't wait. I needed to see Martin Nesbitt now.

# CHAPTER TWELVE

*The Neighbor*

## CLARA

*There is a monster that lurks inside me.*

There must be. No one can kill their husband without something evil somewhere deep inside their soul…

With all the chaos of the last couple days, the missing girl and the bloody scene, I'd forgotten to lay flowers on Annie's grave.

It was a tiny marker, just a small wooden cross at the base of the property. Along the tree line, where the sun cast a narrow pocket of shadows between the trees and the field. This was where Annie liked to play when she was alive. She'd bring her dolls and her ducks, and she'd sit in that shadow, pretending no one could see her but me.

There was a reason she enjoyed "hiding" so much. Like me, she was afraid of her father. Andy had never laid a hand on the girl during those first couple years of her life, but she had often seen us fighting. She'd seen the way he'd laid into her sister, Krissy, screaming and whipping her whenever she'd done something he didn't like.

Despite everything, I still loved my family. I'd wanted Andy to change. I'd thought that if he just quit that drinking, he might be a better father. A better husband. There were moments—moments when he seemed like the man I married... seconds within the day, like when we were watching Seinfeld reruns and we'd laugh so hard our bellies hurt. I'd glance over at his laughing side profile and there he'd be—eighteen-year-old Andy, reincarnated, cutting up and having fun. Or sometimes, I'd expect him to get angry about something, like when I popped a hole in my tire, but then he'd stay perfectly calm and know just what to do.

He stopped drinking for a while, but that was only after it was too late. After he'd killed my Annie.

By all accounts, what happened that day was just a freak accident. Horses are wild and sometimes they get scared. Annie was too young to ride. When the horse got spooked, the fall was just too high. That girl held onto life for a few hours, but then her tiny body couldn't sustain those types of injuries.

While I held my daughter's cold, broken body in my arms at the hospital, Andy was down at the pub, that bastard.

He swore it was an accident, that he was holding her up there gentle-like around the waist, and then the horse saw a fox and took off...that was his story.

*But I know the truth.* He was angry that day. Angry at me for calling him a bad father and determined to watch after Annie all day on his own to prove me wrong. I tried to come out, tried to watch them, to take care of my child, but he yelled for me to go back inside the farmhouse. *I can watch my own daughter, dammit! Better than you can, you mean old bitch*—those were his words that day. Made me nervous, leaving her alone with him, but then again, there was this niggly, nasty part of me that wondered if he was right. I didn't give him enough credit. I never let him watch the girls. And he blamed me for his drinking. Blamed me for how the farm was going under. *You're not the girl you used to be*, he said. *You changed. You made me depressed. You drove me to drink, you terrible woman.*

I was standing at the kitchen sink. Krissy was sitting on the floor by my ankles. Such a needy child, she was just like Annie, always desperate to be close to me even though she was almost ten at the time.

Krissy was coloring in that book of hers, hair swooped around her face like a shield. That's when I heard Andy outside yelling. Not screaming for help but shouting in anger. I recognized that sound. Had heard it before. Heard it so many times…Little Annie was throwing a tantrum again. She was only three, and any time she would go near the barn, she'd cry and scream to ride the horse.

By the time I made it to the back door, I saw him yank her off her feet and toss her on the horse's back. I couldn't hear his words. But I imagined him saying exactly this: "There, you little brat! Just ride the damn thing! Are ya happy now?"

Time slows down. It flexes and bends. It taunts me in my sleep. Oh, how I fucking hate time.

I ran. Hard as I could, I took off across the field toward that horse.

Here's the strange thing: Annie wasn't screaming on the back of that horse. She was *laughing*, wild and excited. Oh, how that girl loved horses…

But then her face changed. That look—*that look*, I'll never forget…it haunts me when I'm asleep. It haunts me when I'm awake.

Eyes wide, her mouth in a troubled *O*. For a second, her eyes met mine. They were confused. Pleading. *Please help me, mommy*, that's what those eyes were saying…

Her eyes begged for me to save her. But then she fell, and her body shattered when it hit the ground.

# CHAPTER THIRTEEN

## *The Cop*

## ELLIE

My personal cell phone chimed on the dash as I veered right onto Meadow Lane. Frustrated, I whipped my cruiser to the side of the silent street. Street lamps glowed hazy and orange overhead, but the houses, despite their whimsical Victorian designs, were quiet and dark.

"Officer James here," I huffed into the phone, instantly realizing that I'd answered my personal phone the way I normally answered the on-call line.

"Good! I was hoping you'd answer," Sergeant DelGrande wheezed into the phone. "You're on your way to see Mr. Nesbitt, aren't you? I just got off the phone with Chad."

Rolling my eyes, I scanned the houses on the right side of the street. I had to be close. The mailbox beside me was 603. Martin Nesbitt lived in 609.

"I am."

"Roland and Mike with you?" he asked.

"Of course not. They stayed behind in the hotel. Roland's probably drinking. Are you surprised?"

"Turn around, Ellie, and go back to the hotel. And call me from your room when you get there. I know the guys give you a hard time, but they're your partners. And you need back-up. You can go first thing in the morning," he said, his voice suddenly deep and serious.

I wanted to argue, but he had a good point. Barging in there alone was probably a bad idea. I couldn't take the risk of shooting another man on the job, deserved or not. But Nova or Lily might need my help at this very moment…

"But what if she's in there, sarge? What if he's hurting that little girl? We missed her call! Maybe we could have stopped her from being murdered."

"But we don't know that she was killed, now do we? The blood we found belonged to a god damned cow. And I did an NCIC on her. Nova Nesbitt has a record. Maybe she staged this whole thing. Maybe she's running in the opposite direction with the girl. She could be in South Carolina by now for all we know. We have to handle this carefully."

Damn. He was right. But still…I couldn't shake the feeling that she was inside that house. "There's a reason she was so scared. He has something to hide. I won't know what that something is till I talk to him."

"Talk to him in the morning with your partners. You're only a few hours away from daylight, anyway. Go sleep and then you can go back. Promise me you will wait, okay?"

"I promise," I groaned, hanging up. I dropped the phone on the passenger seat and gripped the wheel with both hands. I tried not to clench my teeth, but I couldn't help myself. By the time this case was over, I'd need to see a dentist.

Before I could change my mind, I nudged my cruiser door open and stepped out into the street.

It won't hurt to take a quick look at the house. Then I'll go back to the hotel, I decided.

The wind was vicious as I crossed in front of my cruiser and stepped onto the sidewalk. I didn't have a jacket, so I tucked my head down to my chin as I moved beneath the shadowy trees that lined the houses on Meadow Lane.

As I stole a glance up at the houses, the first words that came to mind were "old money". These houses looked like family heirlooms, the kind that people could afford to fix up and take care of.

I counted the house numbers on the mailboxes, finally approaching a baby blue Victorian house. 609 Meadow Lane.

Remembering the rundown cabin on Appleton Farm, it was hard to believe that Nova Nesbitt had traded this to move to Northfolk. The two towns couldn't be any more different from each other. Northfolk was a poor mountain town and Granton was a rising American suburb. It looked like the perfect place to raise a child. The fact that Nova didn't want that further confirmed my theory that she feared the man who lived here.

She reminded me of Mandy Clark; she too had been so desperate and fearful that day…but I hoped finding Nova didn't lead me into making another mistake.

Sarge was right; I needed to bring my partners with me. But I found myself scooting in closer, staring at the hulking house before me…Was there a killer inside?

The house was surrounded by a wrought-iron fence. Several lights were on, upstairs and down, and as I peered closer through the grates, I realized that the house was actually sectioned off into apartments. But which one did Martin and Nova live in?

In the dim gray light, I looked for movement behind the windows. Was he in there somewhere, hiding Nova? I considered Lily Nesbitt. Was she behind these walls, too, just a few feet away from safety?

It looked like there were individual mailboxes and name plates on the far right and left-hand entrances to the house. I moved up and down the sidewalk, trying to read them in the dark. It was pointless. I couldn't see a damn thing out here and I needed to go back now...

I was just about to walk away when the on-call cell phone buzzed loudly in my pocket. I whipped it out and silenced it. Damn you, sarge. He'd probably tried my personal phone to make sure I was headed back to the hotel, and when I didn't answer, he'd called the on-call phone.

I started walking back toward my car, so I could call him back, and that's when I saw the black Chevy Silverado parked on the opposite side of the street. Clara Appleton had said she'd seen a big black truck pull in during the early morning hours before Nova had gone missing, I recalled.

I looked left and right to make sure no one was watching, then I crossed the street. The windows in the truck were dark, and it sat so high up off the ground I couldn't see inside.

Screw it. I placed my right foot on the nerf bar and pushed off the pavement with the other foot. I squinted through the driver's side window, then lost my footing and had to kick off the ground again. The front cab looked neat and clean. In the back, I was disappointed not to see a car seat, or anything to indicate that he'd transported Lily Nesbitt in this car.

But suddenly, something on the back floorboard caught my eye.

Breathless, I looked left and right again, making sure I remained unseen. Then I propped both feet on the nerf bar, cupped my hands around my face, and peered into the backseat of what I presumed was Martin Nesbitt's truck. My jaw tightened with fear.

A pair of little girl's shoes were laying limply on the floor in the back. They were orange and sparkly.

# CHAPTER FOURTEEN

## The Neighbor

### CLARA

In the highest and most exposed part of the field, I walked to see my Annie. Her melodic laughter whistled through the trees. As I knelt down at the tree line, in front of her tiny grave marker, I could almost feel her standing over my shoulder, watching me with a curious, accusatory smile. *Why, mama? Why did you let me fall?*

The fall had killed her. But Andy had facilitated the fall. Ultimately, though, I was responsible. I was her protector. Her *mother*. I should have dug my toes into the dirt, held my ground. Never should have left her with that man. I knew better, and that's why I'd been so worried in the first place when he'd taken her out there…

Ten years—that's how long I waited to kill him. After Annie died, he eventually went back to his old ways—drinking and screaming. Setting the emotional tone in our family. I imagined our house was made of cards. One wrong move, and the whole thing would come tumbling down…

I moved out of our bedroom and slept with Krissy, never leaving her side, even when she was older. She thought I was overprotective, sure, but she and I both knew the real reason. I couldn't stand to lose another daughter.

I stopped fighting with Andy. If he yelled or stomped, I grew quiet. I stared at him with such viciousness sometimes that I think it scared him. Hell, it scared *me*. There's anger and then there's *anger*, the kind of fury that burns deep inside your chest and has no place to go. Sometimes, I wondered if actual steam was emitting from my ears and nose.

Andy took to leaving the house for long bouts of time—either on drinking benders or running around with that mistress of his. I fantasized about killing him so many times, but I *didn't*...I didn't think I had it in me.

After Krissy left, I gave him most of our savings and told him to go stay with his mistress. I thought he'd put up more of a fight than he did, but he didn't. He left. I thought he'd left for good...

When he showed back up, he didn't beg me to take him back and promise to change his drinking, cheating ways...he *told* me he was moving back in. He also told me that he blew through the savings I gave him.

It's strange how when you live with someone abusive, you get so used to it. What's also strange is how quickly you become repelled by men like that once you escape...so, when he turned back up and he raised his fist...I raised a metal shovel and brought it down over his head.

I didn't mean to kill him. That initial smack was an accident... it was self-defense. But I just kept going...I wish I could say that it felt awful. *Unnatural*. But it didn't. It felt like I was finally doling out justice for Annie.

Maybe his evil and meanness slithered out from his body and was absorbed into my own.

A monster lurks inside me. Or maybe *I* am the monster. Maybe I always have been...

Every time I close my eyes, I can feel that shovel in my palm...I can see the red river of blood engulfing his entire face...

"I got you something, angel eyes." I blinked back tears and pressed a hand on my daughter's flimsy marker. It was all I could afford at the time, with the farm going under, and after a while, I grew used to it, not wanting to replace the marker. It was silly—I was worried that if I disturbed it and put up a new one, she might not come back. That her ghost might become lost to me...

In my hand, I held a pack of cheap plastic toys, the kind you can get for a few dollars. Wasn't much, but I'd seen it on the shelf at Dollar Tree, and I'd spotted tiny black horses mixed among the sheep and chickens in the pack. My hands shook as I scooped the horses out, one by one. There were six of them in all. Tenderly, I lined them up on the grass in front of Annie's marker.

That damn horse. Its name was Midnight, a name we let Krissy choose. Should have been mad at the horse, but I couldn't bring myself to get angry at an animal. Annie loved him. We took her to the zoo in St. Paul once, and instead of being interested in the real animals, she was drawn to a sparkly old carousel. Cost a dollar each time you rode. There were at least a dozen horses, with elaborate roses carved on their saddles and manes. She chose the plain black one without a saddle. Looking back, I wonder if she somehow knew a plain black horse would go and kill her...

After the accident, Andy had put that beautiful creature down. I locked Krissy and I in my bedroom and turned on Mickey Mouse to drown out the sound of gunfire when he did it...

"Clara?" Startled, I jerked my head around, surprised to see Sergeant DelGrande standing in the field behind me. It was early, barely daylight.

He was standing with his legs apart, clutching his hat to his chest. His hair was thinner and grayer than it used to be and for the first time, I noticed the thickness of his jowls and the drooping of his shoulders. He'd always been such a kind man. Never could understand why he liked to hang around with Andy.

"Sorry to interrupt you, but we need to talk about something important," he said, solemnly. My heart fluttered in my chest.

# CHAPTER FIFTEEN

*The Cop*

## ELLIE

The entrance to the Nesbitt unit was in the back of the house. I hadn't slept all night. The first thing I did when I saw the shoes was call Sergeant DelGrande back. He'd managed to wake up Judge Horrace and get a warrant issued based on what I found in the truck.

"What if he'd been out there, Ellie? What if he'd attacked you?" Sergeant DelGrande had boomed when I told him about what I had found.

"But he didn't, sir."

"But if he had..."

"Then I guess I would have used my service revolver on him." As soon as the words were out of my mouth, I cringed.

I flinched again, recalling the painful silence that followed on the other end of the line...

Roland and Mike came trudging up the sidewalk. I watched a cab pull away from the curb. I could have gone back to the hotel to pick them up, but I hadn't wanted to leave the scene,

81

just in case Martin was inside and tried to run. If he'd noticed my police car out here, or me looking up at the house, he hadn't let on. I hadn't even seen a curtain rustle in there.

The sun was barely up, but Roland looked like death. I wondered how much drinking he'd done last night. I hadn't slept a wink. My head and jaw were throbbing, but at least I was sober.

"You were supposed to wait for us," Roland grumbled, adjusting the belt around his waist. His uniform was wrinkled and a little smelly. I wondered if he was married. I'd never asked him, but I didn't think he was. Mike, on the other hand, had recently gone through a divorce. He was dressed in a button-down shirt and carefully creased slacks. It didn't look like he'd been up all night, drinking like Roland. Well, at least one of them is sensible, I thought.

"Did ya bring the warrant?" I asked Mike. I'd asked Sergeant DelGrande to have it faxed to the hotel.

Roland unfolded a piece of paper from his pocket and shook it at me. "I got it. Chill."

"We should have waited for SWAT," Mike said as we made our way up to the door.

"Yeah, well, who knows how long that would have taken, or if they'd have come at all." I raised my hand, took a deep breath, then knocked on the Nesbitt residence. I noticed a weathered wicker chair on the front porch. No kid toys or bikes, I noted.

Roland leaned over my shoulder and laid his finger down on the bell. "That's enough," I snapped.

The door swung open quickly and I stepped back in surprise. A nicely dressed man with wavy brown hair and bold blue eyes stared out at us with a look of surprise.

"I'm heading out to work. What can I do for you, officers?"

"Martin Nesbitt?" I asked.

"In the flesh," he said, giving me a smile that showed all his teeth. He was younger than I'd imagined, and handsome too. He was wearing a polo and expensive-looking jeans.

82

"We're here to talk about your wife. She's missing. We also have a warrant to search your truck and home," Roland announced. He held up the warrant from Judge Horrace and the local judge in Granton, Judge Percy.

"O-kaaay. But Nova isn't here. Whatever trouble she's into, whatever she did, I'm not responsible. If she ran somewhere, it wasn't back here to me. Trust me."

"When did you see her last?" I asked.

Martin scrunched up his nose, thinking slowly. "It's been almost a week since she left, and to be honest, I'm not upset she's gone."

"Why didn't you respond to my messages I left you? I called a dozen times," I said, confused.

Martin shrugged. "I thought she was probably in the drunk tank or something. I wasn't about to come bail her out, not after I told her to leave."

"Wait. *You* told her to leave?" This story wasn't jiving with the one Nova told me. Either Martin was a liar, or she was. But which one?

"Okay, we get it. You don't give a fuck about your wife. But aren't you just a little worried about your daughter's safety?" Mike asked.

Martin's eyes grew so wide, I thought they might pop from his head. "You're kidding me, right?"

"Sir, we're very serious. Nova reported your daughter missing on Friday, then she went missing herself. We have reason to believe one or both have come to harm," Mike said.

I was growing impatient. Standing on my tiptoes, I tried to look past him into the unit.

Martin took a big step back, nearly stumbling. At first, I thought he was in shock. But then his next words shook me to the core:

"Nova and I don't have a kid together."

# CHAPTER SIXTEEN

**5 years earlier**

*The Mother*

**NOVA**

My eyes absorbed the dingy, gunmetal gray walls. The ceiling looked like Styrofoam, like that stuff they use in elementary school classrooms. I stared until my eyes crossed and my vision grew blurry, trying to ignore the fact that my legs were spread apart, and my feet were in stirrups.

"You'll feel a slight bit of pressure, and this might be cold," Rachel warned, inserting the ultrasound camera. I pinched my eyes shut, feeling violated even though this sort of thing was supposed to be standard.

"Okay, I can see the baby now. Let me snap some pictures, and I'll be able to tell you if it's a boy or a girl."

"I d-don't w-want to know this time." As a child, I'd developed a horrible stutter. But in my teens, I had been lucky enough to work with a speech therapist at my local high school. The embarrassing stutter was all but gone by the time I met Martin. Then, it had started up again.

Rachel, a local midwife, was crouched on a stool between my legs. The camera probe didn't hurt, but it reminded me of Matthew, my little boy.

I'd spent the first twenty weeks of my pregnancy counting down the days until I could find out the baby's sex. And when I learned it was a boy, I was ecstatic.

I loved the baby in my belly right from the start. They say you can't feel the baby move until you're at least sixteen weeks along in your pregnancy, but I swear I started feeling Matthew kick around week ten. He was an energetic baby, always flipping, waking me up at night. He gave me indigestion. It was weird, but we had this connection only shared by us...Martin couldn't touch it or take it away, even if he tried.

Then Matthew died when I was twenty-two weeks along, less than a week after learning his sex. And lying here now, in this awful, stuffy room, I felt like I was betraying Matthew, as well as Martin.

"It's a girl, Nova. A *girl*!" Rachel squealed. She pointed at the ultrasound machine next to her bed. We were in her cramped apartment, which should have felt less clinical and safe...but it didn't.

For the next few minutes, she pointed out the baby's head, heart, and hands. But I didn't hear her, not really. All I could think about was Matthew, my sweet little Matthew. *Why couldn't it be him in my belly?*

Now I couldn't even pretend it was him, reincarnated, because the baby was a girl. I hadn't even realized I'd wanted this baby to be the new-Matthew in my belly until Rachel gave me this news...

*Martin will be thrilled to find out it's a girl.*

My stomach churned, not from the baby but from the realization that she would have it so much harder in life because of her sex.

Martin would have mistreated his son. *But a girl?*

*He's really going to fuck her up…*

For the first time since finding out I was pregnant again, I placed a hand on my stomach and really considered the future with this new baby.

*Will this one last, or will I lose it again? And if she does make it out of the womb, will she be better off even though her father is a monster?*

"Please d-don't tell anyone I was here," I said, using a towel to wipe up some of the watery gel between my thighs from the probe.

Rachel pushed the machine back and leaned on the edge of the bed. She opened her mouth, then closed it. Finally, she said, softly, "Does he really believe the last ultrasound caused the miscarriage? I could talk to him, explain…"

"N-no. Please, Rachel. He knows I came to see you to get measured, b-but I promised no ultrasound."

"I understand." She smiled, encouragingly. "Congratulations on your little girl. I'm excited to deliver this baby."

I smiled and nodded, but I couldn't look her in the eye. If this baby made it to term, she wouldn't be delivering it. My little girl would have to come into this world all on her own, with only me as her guide.

# CHAPTER SEVENTEEN

*The Neighbor*

## CLARA

"A warrant? That really necessary?" My breath became lodged in my throat and my stomach did a few somersaults.

*A warrant.*

"Not as long as you're okay with it. I promise we'll try not to disturb your property. We need permission for the cadaver dogs to search," Sergeant DelGrande explained.

*Cadaver dogs.*

"You really think someone had enough time to kill my tenant and bury the body, too? That seems a little far-fetched, you know?" We were standing on my front porch now, my mind still back at the barn. Specifically, it was stuck in the hidey hole with my husband's rotting corpse inside. *Cadaver dogs.*

No way could I let them search my side of the property, but if I refused, then they'd just get that warrant.

"We didn't find anything to indicate that a body was buried on the property, but there was a small hole, a couple feet deep near an elm tree in the woods behind the cabin. We're willing to give the dogs a try even if they can't produce results. We're trying to find out what happened here, Clara. A little girl's life could be at stake."

"I don't understand. How's it work?" I asked, my voice coming out shakier than I wanted it to.

"The dogs are attracted to chemical compounds, particularly putrescine and cadaverine. When someone dies, they release chemicals in the air…well, you don't need to know all that. But, my point is, the dogs pick up on the smell of death. Even if there's not a body around, they'll react if a death occurred in a certain place and we need to know if it did. The dogs can find the tiniest things, small bones or even bits of tissue…and we need something to go on." Sam cleared his throat and went on, "Most likely, if the dogs do react, it will be inside the rental house. That's where the teeth were found. That's where the struggle most likely occurred. But, since you're the owner of this land and the cabin on it, I must have your permission," he further explained.

"So, you won't disturb my side of the land, the farm or my house, that right?"

"Not unless the dogs pick up on something, and surely, they won't pick up on anything here." As soon as the words were out of his mouth, I could tell he wanted to reel them back in. He covered his mouth with his hand. "I'm sorry, Clara. I'm such a moron sometimes. I didn't even think about…about…"

"Annie. My daughter's name was Annie," I said, my mouth twisted up with pain. I don't know what it is with people and death—it's like they're afraid to say her name, or to bring her up to me. But that part hurts even more. She was my daughter and it kills me that I don't get to talk about her.

"Annie, yes. And she's buried on the property, over by the marker you were sitting at earlier, correct?"

I nodded stiffly. "Annie died near the barn. Right by it. Her grave's only a few yards away from there. I will let the dogs come if it will help that family, but I don't want them anywhere near

Annie's grave or the barn. Can you make sure of that, Sam? It's where she died…it's her final resting place…I just don't want it disturbed, is all."

"I'll talk to the dogs' handler and make sure he knows that those areas are off limits. It's been so long since Annie's death, that I doubt they'd be able to pick up on the scent of…"

"Her corpse," I finished for him, with a bitter trace in my voice.

Sam squeezed his lips together. "Yes. I think they are usually better at finding fresh bodies. So, you're okay with this then?"

Suddenly, he reached out and squeezed my hand. The gesture felt odd, and strangely, painful. I fought the urge to yank my hand away from him.

"They'll be here in about an hour." Sam tipped his hat in an old-fashioned gesture, then turned to go.

"Can I ask you something else? Why aren't y'all going after the husband? It's usually the husband, you know?"

"Oh, we are. A few of my officers are in Granton right now searching the husband's place. If he's guilty we'll find out soon enough, but we need to process this scene properly, too."

I nodded, a rush of relief rolling through me. As I watched his police car back out and disappear down the steep mountain road, an odd sense of calm washed over my body.

If they find Andy's body, then so be it. There's nothing I can do at this point. I might go to prison for killing him, but I feel like I'm living in prison already.

And if going to jail was the price I had to pay, then I could live with that. Because what happened to Annie couldn't be undone. It was too late to save my daughter. The least I could do was help Lily Nesbitt.

# CHAPTER EIGHTEEN

*The Cop*

**ELLIE**

In grade school, I had a friend named Priscilla Todd. We became instant mates after she defended me from a fourth grader who said my belly was "pokey" and suggested to the entire lunchroom that I was pregnant with Mr. Hammond's love child. I was only in third grade at the time. The whole thing was ridiculous, I know that now, but at the time, I was mortified. Not because of Mr. Hammond, but because of the curl of baby fat around my midsection. I'd never really paid attention to it before. But Priscilla Todd came to my rescue. She followed that bully all the way to her table, then right before she sat down, knocked her lunch from her hands by smacking the bottom of the tray. Mashed potatoes and lime green Jell-O exploded in her face, and the lunch room erupted with laughter. The only one still thinking about my pokey stomach was me. After that, Priscilla and I became best friends. I trusted her with my secrets and fell in love with our friendship. It wasn't until fifth grade that she told me about the cancer. We were sleeping over at my house and it was nearly three o'clock in the morning when she told me. My best friend was dying. At first, I thought it was a joke. But then her face crumpled, and we spent the entire night crying in each other's arms. Over the next few years, we skipped classes together, got suspended together, and spent every waking moment side by side. We knew each other. Like, *really* knew each other, in that bone-deep way only best friends can. What did it matter if I got a few Fs? After all, my friend would be dead soon. I just wanted to be by her side, at all costs. It wasn't until we got into a fight over a boy in eighth grade that she told me the truth. The whole cancer thing had been a lie. A ploy to garner attention from her classmates, and me. I tried to forgive her but discovered I could not. Because it wasn't the lie that bothered me, it was how she told it. I couldn't forget the look of pure agony on her face as she confessed she was dying in fifth grade. She carried on with that lie for years and years, and that scared the hell out of me. That I could know someone so well and also, not know them at all.

So, as I stood there, on the threshold of Martin Nesbitt's home, I didn't believe the words coming out of his mouth. As soon as he realized we were being serious, the color drained from his face.

He looked and sounded sincere. But so had Priscilla when she'd spun her lie…

"Why would she say we had a daughter when we don't? I'm starting to get really worried now. Maybe she's had some sort of schizophrenic episode…"

"Does your wife have a history of schizophrenia, Mr. Nesbitt?" Studying his face, I kept trying to gauge how sincere he was.

Martin swayed over to a sleek, funky-shaped chair and fell back in it. "No, she doesn't. Well, she was pregnant several years ago. We lost the baby."

Roland raised one eyebrow at me.

"How exactly did she lose the baby?" I pressed.

Martin shrugged. "I wish I knew. Just one of those freak things, I guess. Her body rejected the baby. I was kind of relieved. I mean, at first, I was excited about the baby, but then it almost seemed like fate…I'm a realtor and at the time, Nova was talking about going back to school to get a degree. She was depressed at first, for a few months, but then we moved on. We talked about trying again in the future, but it never happened. Want the truth? After that, she became possessive. Controlling. She definitely wasn't the sweet woman I married. Maybe losing the baby made her lose her mind…"

Mike looked over at me and raised his eyebrows, as though he were wondering the exact same thing. I had to admit, this picture Martin was painting of Nova was completely different to the woman I'd met, and their stories weren't jiving at all. Sure, Nova had seemed nervous and frightened. But not delusional…

"Or maybe she just wanted to get back at me." Martin narrowed his eyes and smirked. For a moment, I thought I saw his cool façade slipping…

"Get back at you for what exactly, Mr. Nesbitt?" I pushed.

"For wanting out of our marriage. She knew I wanted to end things," he said, shrugging.

"If so, that still doesn't explain the blood and teeth we found in her cabin," I said. But after I said it, I remembered what Chad said, about the blood being non-human. Could Nova have staged some sort of scene to get back at her ex…? That seemed far-fetched…but with her criminal record and the phony blood and her husband's reports…it was hard not to wonder.

"You said blood and teeth?" Martin stood up from his chair, running his fingers through his hair as he paced around in circles.

"Is my wife dead?" He stopped moving. His chin trembled, and he looked about as sincere as it gets.

But still, there are always Priscillas in this world, the chip on my shoulder whispered.

"We don't know, Martin. That's why we're here. We're trying to find your wife and daughter." Roland coughed when he got to the last part.

"But I don't know where she is! And like I said, I don't have a daughter with anyone!"

"Okay, Mr. Nesbitt, calm down. Right now, what I'm going to have you do is take a seat right there." I pointed at the same chair he'd collapsed in earlier. The living room was swanky and neat, like your quintessential bachelor pad. My eyes traveled around the room. Again, like when I'd searched the cabin, I noticed how kid-free it seemed. My eyes were drawn to a small scattering of photos on the wall. Martin and Nova making a toast at their wedding. Martin and Nova perched on the back of a boat. No pictures of children.

Martin sat down, but he perched on the edge of the seat, looking nervous.

"This shouldn't take too long," Mike assured him, and I shot him a warning look.

"Martin, there are a pair of shimmery orange sneakers in your backseat. The same description Nova gave us when she reported the child was missing. How do you suppose those got there if you don't have a daughter?" I asked him.

I was standing behind him as I asked the question, and he whipped around in a flash. "What the hell are you talking about?" Thick eyebrows bunched together, and I noticed him gripping the arms of the chair. His knuckles went pearly white, thick blue veins bulging out of his forearms. There was a twinge of anger in his big blue eyes.

"When your wife reported your daughter missing, she gave us a description of the shoes Lily was wearing."

"Lily?"

"Your daughter," I said, through clenched teeth.

"*Supposed* daughter," Mike corrected, and I gave him an ugly stare.

"A pair of shoes that fit that description are lying on the back floorboard of your truck. Who do they belong to?" I asked.

"You must be talking about someone else's truck. There aren't any shoes in mine. Are you sure...?"

"Is this your truck?" Taking out my cell phone, I punched a few buttons and pulled up my camera roll. I'd taken nearly a dozen pics of Martin's truck and I'd tried to take as good of a shot as I could get of the shoes, despite the heavily tinted windows. I handed him the phone, showing him a side shot of the exterior on his truck. He stared at it for a few seconds, before nodding.

"That's definitely mine. But I don't know anything about those shoes, officer."

"What about a toy rabbit? Nova found a stuffed rabbit in her daughter's bed. Did you put it there?"

Martin shifted around in his seat, uncomfortably. "Listen, Nova doesn't have a daughter and neither do I. And I didn't even know where she was until now. I don't know anything about a stupid little bunny."

I froze, remembering what Nova said he called his daughter. *Little Bunny.*

Roland was already moving around, inspecting the kitchen, but I couldn't take my eyes off Martin Nesbitt. "I never told you the rabbit was little. Do you like little bunnies, Martin?"

Those wild eyebrows shot up again and I could see his jaw flexing through his cheeks.

"Jesus. I just assumed since you said it was a 'toy rabbit' that it must be small. Sorry, okay? I don't know anything about a rabbit. And the shoes, Nova must have put them there. Or I guess they could belong to my little niece, Kailey, but she hasn't ridden in my truck in a long time." He held his hands up, shaking his head. "Do I need to call a lawyer? It seems like your minds are already made up here, and I'm starting to feel uncomfortable."

"That's your right to seek counsel, sir," Roland called from the kitchen. He pointed his finger at Martin, then placed his other

94

finger to his lips and looked at me. He was right. No reason to set off our suspect just yet. If he was guilty, we would find evidence to support it.

"I'm sorry, Mr. Nesbitt. If it seems like I'm being hostile, it's only because I want to find your wife. And frankly, if I was confused before I got here, I'm really baffled now. You see, I'm new at this. And the last thing I want is a dead kid on my hands. Do you understand my predicament?" I blinked slowly and forced myself to smile with all my teeth. If I had to play nice to keep the lawyers at bay, I would do it. Let him think I'm stupid, if that's what it takes, I decided.

Martin gave me a sly smile. His eyes flickered down to my breasts then back up to my face. "I get it. I don't have a daughter. However, I would like to find Nova, so that I can file for divorce. She's obviously lost her mind." A chill ran up my spine at the slight change in the tone of his voice.

"Mike, will you stay here with Mr. Nesbitt, please? I'm going to look around really quick. Just to be thorough." I smiled phonily at Martin again.

After Mike nodded, I made a beeline for the hallway that ran off the kitchen. My stomach was curling. Martin Nesbitt was one slick bastard and I didn't buy his story, not even for a second. My gut was telling me not to.

# CHAPTER NINETEEN

**4 years earlier**

*The Mother*

## NOVA

The first time I saw him, he had been standing by a pool table in Bill's Bowling Alley. He wore jeans and an army green hoodie. The hood was up, concealing his hair and the sides of his face. His hands casually tucked in his pockets, he seemed quiet, his eyes flickering up to meet mine. A slow, trickster smile played at the corner of his lips before his eyes dropped back down to the floor.

He wasn't playing pool. Like me, he'd been dragged along with his friends. Mine were Louise and Kerry, two girls I'd met at Sunny's, the place where I waitressed a few nights a week. They were closer to each other than they were to me, but they'd just kept on asking me to go out with them. After a while, I ran out of excuses.

But on that night things were different. Surprisingly, I was enjoying myself. It was the flutter in my stomach, the tiny burst of adrenaline that let me know I was attracted to Martin. For most of the night, we didn't even speak. Both introverts, it took nearly a dozen drinks between us to knock the walls down and help us loosen up. By the time the lanes went dark and the bar closed, we'd forgotten all about our friends. We were in our own little cocoon and I couldn't have shaken off that buzz of excitement, even if I'd wanted to. Faces around us, they all looked blurry and nondescript. No one else mattered but Martin and me.

I'd like to say it was "love at first sight", but it was more like a craving. We had to have each other, and we both knew it before we even spoke.

There was something feral in the way he fucked. It wasn't rough; more like, intense. Martin fucked like a frenzied animal, like he'd been waiting for this moment all his life, like if he didn't have me he would die.

My friends loved him, but they still thought it was all too soon when I announced that we were getting married. It was crazy and rash, but I'd never been one to look ahead. When I was in the moment—*that* moment, *that* high—I couldn't even fathom what the come down would feel like, almost like I was so high that I truly believed I'd never come down.

Martin was my drug of choice, and I craved him right from the start. Even the idea of getting married turned me on, and not in the romantic sense of the word. When I thought about marrying Martin, I thought about garter belts and lingerie. Steamy sex in Fiji and fucking on the plane ride home.

I didn't think about all the other stuff, what comes after the high. I didn't anticipate what would happen—Martin turning into someone I didn't recognize.

Now I gauge Martin's moods by the rise and fall of his shoulders. I know what sort of day he's going to have, and what sort of day that means for me, within seconds of him waking up. At first, I thought it was just intuition, or maybe some sort of psychic ability springing to life, but then I realized it was the little things, things I'd barely even noticed, that alerted me to his moods.

The way his feet hit the hard wood floor beside our bed—if his feet smacked the floor heavily and if he walked just a slight bit faster than usual to the bathroom when he first got up, that meant he was angry already. Maybe it was from bad dreams, or maybe he was just bad in general, I don't know. But he woke up pissed off at the world, and I suffered because of it.

When I was little, I was afraid of the dark. My father refused to play into my fears, not even granting me the luxury of a night light, or light from the hallway bathroom. One night I asked him, "How c-come you're not af-fraid of the d-dark, d-daddy?"

"Because the dark's afraid of me!" he'd cackled, body bubbling forward as he laughed and laughed. There was booze on his breath that night, and most nights, really. But I'll never forget those words. Martin and Dad, they weren't afraid of things, things were afraid of them.

If Martin sounded angry when he woke up, I busied myself immediately and tried to stay out of his way until his mood relaxed. I tried to coordinate the baby's sleep schedule, so she'd sleep right through his morning routine. The boy from the bowling alley was gone, replaced by this edgy, unhappy man I felt afraid of.

"Your fucking half-sister woke me up! Why is she calling my phone?" He threw his cell phone at me, causing me to jerk in surprise. The cell phone, though light, stung as it smacked my left breast and clattered to the floor. I knew before he turned it over that the screen was going to be cracked. My own screen had cracked much the same way.

"Great! Now look what that bitch made me do." Martin snatched up his shattered phone from the floor, pivoted on one foot, and threw it as hard as he could at the living room wall. This time, it cracked and split. I stared at the broken pieces on the floor and I recognized the slippery slope that was Martin

Nesbitt. Now that his phone was broken, he wouldn't be able to call me from work. And since I would be home alone while he worked, he'd tear the house apart when he got back, looking for "evidence" that I'd been cheating. It was a slippery slope indeed.

Suddenly, he wrapped his arms around my shaking body, gathering me into him. The walls were caving in around me, the world spinning on its axis…I crumpled into him. Not because I wanted him to comfort me, but because I wanted this tantrum to end before Lily woke up.

Lily…my perfect, beautiful miracle. The one good thing in my life. How could I protect her from this? *How?*

"I'm sorry for throwing the phone at you, sweetie. She just kept calling and calling! She knows I need my sleep. What do you think she wants this time?" The room swayed back and forth as I struggled to think of a reason. Most likely, she was calling him because she couldn't reach me. I didn't answer her calls anymore. If I did, Martin asked questions and got jealous; it simply wasn't worth it.

"Can't you text her and tell her to fuck off?" He gripped my shoulders now, squeezing tighter and tighter as he spoke. "If you don't tell her, I will. And trust me, you don't want that. You know how I feel about her."

Martin stormed off, leaving me to pick up the pieces of his phone while he got ready for work. I'd already checked to make sure he had socks and underwear, his clothes laid out straight. Sometimes I missed something, and he didn't yell or get upset, but then sometimes he got very angry. I'd started taking precautions, making sure ahead of time that I'd minimized anything that could set off the descent down his slippery slope.

If he had everything he needed, and nothing pissed him off, then he'd leave for work on time, and I wouldn't cry for hours afterwards.

But today, was not going to be one of those days.

"These are the old socks! The ones with the holes in them!" I heard him shouting from our bedroom. I flinched as dresser drawers flew open and shut. Then a sharp bang from where he'd probably kicked my bookshelf again.

I heard several soft thuds. My books were falling. *Yep, I was right about the shelf.*

You see, it had nothing to do with intuition. It was learned behavior. *I'm no better than that stupid dog that Pavlov taught to salivate when it heard a bell.*

I'd learned to duck and dodge Martin's mood swings by staying one step ahead of him. But there were some things I didn't plan for well enough—like when he stole my birth control pills and got me pregnant on purpose or when he forced me to deliver my own child on the bathroom floor.

# CHAPTER TWENTY

*The Cop*

## ELLIE

Follow your intuition. Trust that sixth sense of yours—that's what my female instructor from the academy told me when I was doing a simulation search and seizure drill. *It doesn't always make sense at the time but trust those tiny signals your body gives you. Fear is a friend you don't want to get rid of*, she'd said.

I never forgot those words. But even though I wanted to listen, to follow my gut this time, I just couldn't. There was nothing in Martin Nesbitt's apartment or truck, besides the shoes he now claimed belonged to his niece, that would indicate a child lived there. The bedspread in the master bedroom was neat, with gold-colored embroidery and mountains of pillows at the head of it. There was an extra bedroom, but it didn't appear to belong to a child. No kid-sized beds or tiny shoes. No little landmines of toys.

I opened drawers and cabinets. I inspected the bathroom for baby soaps or powders, a miniature toothbrush, anything to make me think a child had been here recently...*nothing.*

There was a his and hers closet in the master; one side held what appeared to be Martin's clothes: fancy silk shirts, polo pants, ties…and the other side was full of women's clothes. I closed my eyes, clenching and unclenching my jaw, trying to melt from the room and remember every detail about Nova when I met with her at the cabin. She was wearing that pink robe and lacy undergarments. She was a handsome woman with a trim figure, and the neat dresses and slacks on the hangers seemed to fit her small frame and style, as far as I could tell. Why did she leave it all behind? I wondered. The fact that she left so much made me believe her story…if she was truly afraid of this man, then she would only grab essentials and go…But where are Lily's things? What sort of motivation would Martin have for covering up his daughter's existence?

"Nova didn't take her clothes with her. Or her shoes," I mumbled, mostly to myself. I stared at the floor of the closet. There had to be fifty pairs of heels and flats and sneakers piled haphazardly on top of each other. No kid shoes, I noted again.

Martin spoke up, startling me. "I'm sure she took some things with her when she left. She has too much to keep track of. I like to spoil the women I'm with, if you know what I mean."

He was standing in the doorframe of the bedroom. He gave me a sideways smile that almost looked seductive.

"Are you telling me you didn't see her leave? I thought you're the one who told her to go? Isn't that what you said earlier?"

"I did tell her to leave. But I never thought she'd actually listen. I was surprised when I came home from work and realized she was gone."

"So, can you give me a list of what you think she took with her? What about her cell phone? Do you have that here?" I knew damn well Nova didn't have her cell phone. That was one of the first things she told me when I came to her house. I remembered that chintzy flip phone she had tucked away in the kitchen drawer.

Martin took slow strides toward me, his eyes focused intensely on mine as he drew in closer. Where the hell are Mike and Roland? I wondered, feeling my back stiffen.

"Your partners went out for a smoke break," Martin said, as though he could read my mind.

I took a step back. Backing myself even further against the closet. I pressed my lips together, mashing my teeth in discomfort. Martin grinned. "I hope you're not afraid of me. I really am a good guy. And I'm telling you the truth, scouts honor." He stuck his arm out and I flinched involuntarily. "Just getting this."

Martin reached across me and into the top of the closet, grabbing something off the shelf. I shuddered as his arm grazed my shoulder. "Here's the cell phone you asked about."

It was a sleek white iPhone, similar to the one I used. I was shaken, but I tried to hide it. I could kill Mike and Roland for leaving me alone in here with him, I thought.

"Thank you." Awkwardly, I took the phone from his hand and pressed the home button. Nothing happened. Martin was still staring at me, making me uncomfortable. There was something odd about his demeanor...not the way a man with a missing wife should act, even if he'd fallen out of love with her.

"It's dead. I can charge it though, if you want me to plug it in. I haven't even looked at it...You probably think I'm a terrible husband, but Nova really was a handful."

"I don't think anything, sir. I'm just trying to figure out where she is, and why she reported a little girl missing who you claim doesn't exist. I'm going to need your cell phone, too, and any other electronics you have in the house."

Martin raised his eyebrows, genuinely surprised. His eyebrows were atrocious—wild and busy, like two fat caterpillars on his face. "Is that really necessary? I need my cell phone for work." There was a slow, steady tick working on his right jaw.

"We'll return it as soon as we can." I stuck my hand out, palm up, waiting for him to turn it over. As he handed me his phone, he held on for a second too long, challenging my eyes with his own. I didn't breathe or blink, I just waited for him to let go. What sort of game is he playing? I wondered. For someone whose wife recently went missing—whether they were on the heels of divorce or not—he shouldn't be acting like this. And the way he seemed to enjoy making me uncomfortable while my male colleagues were out of the room, made me even more suspicious. Martin Nesbitt was covering up something, but what?

"I understand," he said, finally. He let go and internally, I breathed a sigh of relief.

If Martin or Nova had something to hide, their phones were the best place to uncover it.

# CHAPTER TWENTY-ONE

**3 years earlier**

*The Mother*

## NOVA

After a while, they all stopped calling. Even the people who loved me the most, my dad and half-sister, could only take so much of my dodging and ducking.

"Don't ignore them on my behalf. Seriously, babe. Call them. Let them know that you're okay. I don't want to keep you from your family," Martin urged.

*Lies. All lies.*

I was slicing potatoes and onions for soup. Behind me, he rubbed his thumb back and forth across the soft curl of flesh below my hairline. A shiver crawled over my skin, turning my head woolly and warm. *His touch used to bring me pleasure, but now it just creeps me out.*

Moments like these, I couldn't help but roll my eyes at his behavior. If I talked to my family, he punished me for it. But if I chose to ignore them, he encouraged me to reach out. He didn't want me to blame him for the fact that I'd lost touch with them—he wanted me to hate them all on my own.

"O-okay, I will call them t-tomorrow." But that was a lie, too. He didn't want them involved in Lily's life. And because I knew they wouldn't take no for an answer if they knew about her, I'd kept her a secret from them. It was wrong...*so wrong*...but I knew having them around, trying to see Lily, would only make him take out his anger on Lily and me even more.

"Good." Martin flicked my earlobe with his tongue. My body prickled, but I forced a smile anyway.

"Let me cut. I need to get this soup on the stove," I teased, nudging him away with my shoulder. As he left the kitchen, I gripped the handle of the butcher knife until my knuckles turned white. I poked the tip of the knife in the center of the onion's heart.

*How did I become so isolated?*

At one time, I had more friends than I could count. At work and school, I had a small army of girlfriends. And I had aunts and uncles, cousins, my sister and dad...but slowly, all my relationships peeled away like layers on an onion. The stuttering I used to suffer from as a child was back. It was almost like I was getting younger and more vulnerable every day that I spent with him.

Martin seemed to like my family in the beginning. Mostly, my dad and sister because my other relatives weren't around much. Besides a few major holidays, I didn't see my other relatives. But at the wedding...everyone came to that.

The ceremony had been breathtaking, but the day itself was blurry and stressful and *hot*. We got married outside in the middle of July and in my wedding dress, with the long train and itchy Chantilly fabric seared to my skin, I roasted and blistered under the hot summer sun. But I was beaming that day, and so was Martin, and when it came time to leave, I couldn't wait to jump into the back of that limo and strip the heavy parts of my veil and dress away. I wanted to get away from the crowds and the heat...but most of all, I wanted to be with my new husband, our own little love cocoon.

He got in the limo while I gave my family one last round of hugs and kisses, and then I climbed in behind him. When I saw the stone-cold look on his face, my stomach churned with fear. It was one of those phone-rings-in-the-middle-of-the-night-type moments. For a second, I wondered if he'd received some sort of bad news.

"What is it, Martin? What's happened?" I eased myself down on the seat beside him, expecting the worst. His two favorite cousins hadn't attended the wedding. *Did something happen to one of them?* I wondered.

His face was a mask, skin stretched tight against the bone, and he wouldn't even look at me.

"Please, tell me." I put my hand on his shoulder, but he shoved it off. That shove was so shocking, and so unexpected, that my breath caught in my throat for several seconds. *We just got married. Why is he angry with me?* I'd never seen him angry or cold like this before. We'd had a few minor disagreements and one night, we'd had a heated debate about gun control that ended in laughter and sex. *But nothing like this.*

In my mind, I rewound the tape, searching through my vault of memories as I tried to play out the day. *What could I have possibly done to make him act like this?*

"Come on. It's our wedding day. Tell me what's going on." Again, I tried to touch him, and he shoved me off.

"Fine. You know what, Martin? Maybe you should just go on our honeymoon by yourself." The limo hadn't started moving yet, so I reached for the door handle. That's when he grabbed my arm, squeezing the fleshy bit on the bottom so hard that I cried out in pain. As soon as I yelped, he released his grip and burst into tears.

I was so shocked by the painful squeeze and the tears that I sat back down in my seat and just stared at him in wide-eyed horror. The limo lurched forward and through the tinted glass, I watched the rose gardens we'd just got married in melt away. I watched my smiling family and friends dissolve…

"That really hurt." I rubbed my arm, wondering if it would bruise, and watched Martin sob into his hands. I didn't ask him again what was wrong, and I didn't try to touch him. I just watched him cry and felt like crying myself. *What the fuck was going on with my husband? Did he get too drunk during the dinner and toast?* But I'd seen Martin drunk and sick and scared. He'd never reacted like this before. *Never.*

Finally, when he looked up at me, his eyes were red and raw from crying, but at least he didn't look hard or menacing now. He looked like the man I'd married, only distraught.

"It's mom," he choked out the words.

"Oh my god. Is she alright?"

She'd been at the wedding, of course, and I'd talked to her, but not much. I couldn't really talk to any one person for too long, there were just too many people at the ceremony…

"She's okay. Just hurt, that's all. Right before we left, she pulled me aside. I've never seen her look so distraught."

"Why? What happened?" I gasped.

Martin narrowed his gaze at me. "God, I'm trying to tell you, if you'd just let me talk for once. You always interrupt people, you know that? It really bothers me. I'm sure it drives people crazy, not just me."

"It d-does?" I stammered. My old, familiar stutter caught me by surprise. I was stunned by Martin's words. And hurt. My cheeks grew hot with shame.

I liked Martin's mother, but no matter what was wrong with her, it couldn't justify this sort of behavior on his part.

I felt a flash of anger but stayed quiet, waiting for him to explain.

"Like I said, mom's hurt. She was in the bathroom when she

heard your rude-ass aunt and sister talking by the bathroom sink."

I fought the urge to ask, 'which aunt?'. Three of my dad's sisters had been in attendance.

"I know your dad paid for everything. Don't think for even a minute that my mom and I aren't bothered about that fact. If she could have helped pay for it, she would have, Nova."

*Money? This is about money?!* I wanted to scream.

"Your sister was bitching to your Aunt June about how much everything cost and how my mom had barely thanked your dad for it. I guess she wanted my mom to get down on her knees and kiss your dad's fucking feet. They were also making fun of my mom's dress. They said she probably got it off the rack at Walmart. Then my mom came out of the stall and interrupted their bashing session."

My face turned white. I tried to picture my Aunt June and half-sister, Rita, saying those kinds of things. My sister wasn't snobbish, but June kind of was. Maybe together they were being catty. I didn't see any reason for Martin's mom to lie about it, but still, why would they do that on a day like today?

"My mom apologized to them, can you believe that? She actually said that she was sorry for not paying more, then she ran out of there in tears. I didn't see her for hours. She must have been hiding somewhere in the gardens, trying to avoid your family." He hissed out the words 'your family' through his teeth.

"I'm so sorry. I just c-can't believe they would say s-something like that…"

"Oh, so now my mom is a liar?"

"No, of course th-that's not what I'm s-saying." I put my hand on his leg and this time, he didn't push me away. "I'm just shocked, th-that's all. And my heart is broken for your m-mom. What an awful thing for them to say. Martin, I know you're m-mad, but I love you and it's not f-fair to take it out on me. I'm on your

109

side. *You're* my f-family now. We can't turn on each other when b-bad things happen, okay?"

Martin's face turned buttery and sweet, and he smiled. It was *that* smile again, the one I fell in love with on that very first night. "God, I'm such a prick. Your poor arm. I can't believe I grabbed you so hard. I'll never forgive myself. Can you forgive me?" He kissed the sore spot where he'd grabbed me, his lips as soft as butterfly wings.

"Of course, I forgive you, Martin. But please, from now on, let's just talk these things through. You can n-never treat me that way again, do y-you understand?" Adrenaline rushed through my bloodstream, my teeth chattering despite the day's warmth. I was still reeling from how quickly his mood had turned and then turned back...

For a while, things got better again. I almost forgot about the incident completely. Our honeymoon was the best vacation of my life. We hiked and swam. We made love more times than I could count. And when we got back, I didn't talk to my sister for weeks. It was my dad that I finally talked to first, confiding in him about what Martin's mom had heard in the bathroom. Surprisingly, he defended my sister and June, arguing relentlessly that they would never do that to me and that Martin was trying to turn me against my family. *I know a bad guy when I see one. He's shiny and slick, but that's how guys like us appear to outsiders. I know that, because I used to be one*, he said.

By the time I was old enough to not need my father anymore, he had changed his ways. He'd quit drinking and drugging and became a semi-stable figure in my life. My half-sister was younger than me, the product of another romantic encounter with a woman that didn't stick around, and she had always been more willing to forgive our dad.

I was so pissed at him for defending her and talking bad about Martin that I didn't talk to him for months. It was just me and Martin, versus everyone else.

But as time passed, we all sort of made up. I went to visit my sister and invited my dad out for lunch. However, Martin was never the same around them. It was so uncomfortable when we were all together that I tried to avoid too much contact, at least when Martin was around.

But then, it started to seem like there were problems everywhere…my friend Kerry showed up one day when I wasn't home, and Martin said she tried to hit on him. So, no more Kerry. And then my boss at the restaurant, Tom, was an issue too. Martin said Tom was obsessed with me and every time I went to work, Martin would call and call, getting me in trouble at work. Eventually, I gave up my job and most, if not all, of my family and friends.

It wasn't until I was pregnant with Matthew that I realized the problem was Martin. Everyone in my life was perceived as a threat by him, and instead of leaving him or telling him to get over himself, I changed who I was for him. I don't know when I changed—it was gradual, like gaining twenty pounds over a year's time or watching a flower grow.

One day I was a gypsy soul—strong, independent, opinionated, ambitious, worthy—and the next day I was weak and pathetic and stuttering again. I questioned every move I made and tailored who I was to meet Martin's standards. By the time I gave birth to Lily, I had no one left.

*As weak as he thinks I am, I'm about to prove him wrong.*

I chopped the onion into little bits and tossed it into the soup. For hours, I stood there, watching the bubbly broth consume the fleshy onions, making them soft until they disappeared. Like me, they were still there, below the surface, only hiding.

# CHAPTER TWENTY-TWO

*The Neighbor*

**CLARA**

I gripped the iron banister and turned on the basement light. The bulb flickered once, twice, then burned out. I felt my way down the creaky stairs. Let the darkness swallow me whole. I bumped into picture boxes, old books, and tools. I knocked cobwebs out of my face.

I don't know how I found the Maglite, but the flood of sickly yellow light warmed the cold, damp space as I looked around in the dark.

Forty years is a long time, and over the years, I'd accumulated a lot of stuff. Most of it was useless, but not the kind of stuff you want to throw away.

Old photo albums that I'd inherited when my dad, and then my mom, passed on. School papers and science projects from when Krissy was young. Stuff from my own childhood—trophies and badges that belonged to me and my sisters, small tokens of our accomplishments that mama had saved.

Would these same boxes collect dust some day in Krissy's attic or closet? Where does it all end? Is it so important to hang onto everything, the good and the bad?

I didn't want Krissy to inherit all my baggage, so I decided, once and for all, to start throwing some of it out. I couldn't do anything about the body in the barn right now, not with the police searching my property, but I could at least do this...

Opening the mouth of an industrial strength garbage bag, I dumped an entire box of Girl Scout badges inside it. Next, I reached for a dusty, grey tote.

There are things I want to remember and things I want to forget.

If moments of my life could be compiled into a Greatest Hits collection, they'd feature: me, running circles around my high school track, sweat on my face and between my thighs, as mama and daddy cheered for me, their screams so loud that they were all I could hear as I crossed the finish line. Then there's me, getting my diploma and college acceptance. I was the first in my family to graduate from high school. And the night I met Andy at a school mixer. We were two of only thirteen people who showed up. Might as well have been alone, because we danced and talked all night, never taking our eyes off one another. And Krissy. When she was born she was pink and chubby, fuzzy bits of hair on her face and back. I could remember thinking, she is the cutest baby in the whole world, and not just because she's mine. I really believed that, until my Annie was born. She, too, was gorgeous. Like her sister, she clung to me constantly, never wanting to leave my side, even after she could walk. Annie's bowed legs moving in and out, like tiny little butterfly wings. Her smile, so silly and sweet that it brought me to tears when she first learned to do it. And the farm when it was thriving...I loved feeding the chickens and planting crops in the spring. It made me glowing and healthy. These are my Greatest Hits...

Then you strip away those great moments—you're left with all the in between. Annie's accident. Andy's drinking. The venom in his eyes when he was mad. The hurt look on Krissy's face when her father yelled at her just because he was drunk. The way Krissy sunk inside herself after she lost her little sister. The crying. The anger. The way I couldn't be a good mother anymore because half my heart was gone...The way Andy's face caved in, like chopping into a watermelon, when I swung that shovel again and again...oh god, how could I be so stupid? I could have taken the beating—I'd taken many of Andy's beatings before. Or I could have called the cops. Why did I have to strike so hard, and with such vehemence?

I picked up a heavy box of pictures and stumbled over to the open bag, grunting at its weight.

Suddenly, there was a hard, panicked knock upstairs and I dropped the box at my feet. Pictures of Andy and the girls spread out across the floor like a Japanese hand fan. I stared at all their faces, zeroing in on one of my sister. Smudgy faces...smudgy memories...so many mistakes.

My breath became lodged, my throat constricting, as I slowly tiptoed up the stairs. Another loud knock rattled my entire body.

At the top of the stairs, I approached the front door, hugging the wall for support. I needed a cigarette. I needed something to make my blood stop thudding in my ears...

Sergeant DelGrande was at the door. I could see the brim of his hat through the frosted glass, his eyes like two sloppy black holes glaring back at me through the other side.

They'd been out there all day, searching. Searching the farm for clues. I hadn't dared looked, so fearful of what they might find.

He started pounding on the door again. His knock was serious. Frantic.

He knows. They must have found his body...

But what else did they find...?

My hand on the knob, I closed my eyes and remembered one last hit on my soundtrack in life: the first time I saw Nova Nesbitt.

She stepped out of her shimmery, blue car, wind whipping her hair around like a Pantene commercial. It took forever for her to turn around, so I could see her face from my window. Her eyes were blue, so blue they were almost violet. Reminded me of the bluebells that used to bloom in late April at the far-right edge of the field. Nova Nesbitt didn't see me. She couldn't, I was too far away, hidden behind the safety of my own kitchen curtains. But I watched her for several minutes that night. Afterwards, I would try to remember every detail of her face.

# CHAPTER TWENTY-THREE

*The Cop*

**ELLIE**

By the time I slipped out of the Nesbitt residence, my phone was full of missed calls. A few from the sergeant and Chad; the rest from my mom. I'd forgotten all about calling her, like I promised I would when I got to Granton.

Rain drizzled down in a cool mist. It was still too hot for September. I imagined this same street, one month from now, when kids from the neighborhood would walk door to door, offering tricks and asking for treats on Halloween night. Would Lily Nesbitt be among them?

And then the real question: does Lily Nesbitt even exist? I tried to conjure up reasons for a woman to lie, and I couldn't think of any, besides some sort of mental illness or delusional disorder. Remembering how anxious and erratic she seemed, I wondered if I was trying to believe her too much...But there *was* one thing I felt certain of: Martin had something to hide.

Unlike Nova, he had a motive to lie about his daughter—if he'd taken her, or god forbid he'd killed her, then he had every

116

reason to hide the truth. But the birth of a child wasn't something that could easily be covered up. There were birth records and medical history…and that's why I had to dig deeper and look for other people who could shed some light on this for me. People, besides Martin, who knew and understood Nova. People who could verify that she had a child. Someone who could give us an idea of where she might have run off to.

Martin had written down phone numbers for Rita Clause and Reginald McKinley. Rita was Nova's half-sister and Reginald was her father. They lived less than thirty miles away, and only two doors apart from each other, apparently. But first, I wanted to talk to the neighbors. A child was something hard to miss, even if they didn't get out much.

The apartment to the left of the Nesbitts' had a deeper porch, but you wouldn't know it by all the garbage scattered about. I stepped around a broken chandelier that had probably been lovely at one time. Now a long rusty chain sprouted from its top and lay haphazardly across the concrete porch. I side-stepped the chain, squeezing my way up to the door between broken potted plants and a stack of old phone books, the kind with the liberty bells ringing on the top of the page. When my sister and I were little, we used to play this game: pick a letter of the alphabet, run your finger along last names until your finger felt compelled to stop, then call them. Based on their name and the sound of their voice, we had to see who could come up with the most elaborate story to go along with the name/voice. Now, thinking back on it, it seemed pretty lame, but we'd passed hours doing that on long summer days.

Knocking on the screen door, I noticed a faded sign taped to the inside door. The letters were scratchy and old, but I could read it: *Knock loud, drop it at the door, or go away.* I opened the screen and banged the side of my fist on the grimy yellow door, slivers of paint flecking off as I did. It took a few minutes, but a man, wearing too-high trousers and no shirt, finally came to the door. When he asked me what I wanted, I realized he had no teeth.

"Officer James here. Do ya know the couple next door?"

"Huh?" He cupped one hand around his ear and leaned at an awkward angle in the doorway.

I asked him again, only this time my words came out considerably louder.

He nodded, smacking his gums together. "See the husband every day. Martin, his name is. His face pops out at me all over this town. Nice fella."

"What about his wife and daughter? Do ya ever see them outside?" I asked, scooting back an inch and bumping into one of the plants.

"Yeah, every once in a while. Crazy black hair, that one. She's a real looker. You know what I mean?"

"Do you ever see her little girl? Her name is Lily." Again, I wished I had some sort of picture or image to show him.

"Huh? Who?"

Disappointed, I thanked him for his time and stumbled my way off his cluttered porch. In the center of the backyard was a stone bench, with tiny angels playing trumpets carved on the seat of it. Behind it was a large fountain. It was lovely, but overgrown, and the water had all but run dry inside. This would have been a decent place for a child to play. I couldn't imagine one of the neighbors not seeing the mother and daughter together...

Hot pellets of rain trickled down and I ran for the other apartment's porch before I got too wet. The apartment to the right of Martin's was much neater, with a plant box. Big, yellow daisies and violets sprouted from the top of it, and there was a wrought iron table for two right beside it. I knocked softly on the door, squeezing excess water from my ponytail as I waited. By now, the heavy makeup I'd put on yesterday was probably streaking my cheeks and clumping in the corners of my eyes.

When the door crept open, I instantly smelled marijuana

rolling out through the crack. A big brown eye looked out at me. "What's the problem, officer?"

"Hey, I'm trying to find out some information about the little girl and her mom who lived next door. Lily and Nova Nesbitt. Can ya talk?"

"I don't really know them, sorry." A nose and mouth appeared to go along with the eye, and the girl looking out at me barely looked twenty.

"Look, I don't care about the pot. I need to ask ya a couple questions though, if that's okay."

The young woman opened the door wide enough, just enough so she could scurry through it. She had a cute haircut, shaved on one side and longer on the other, and a delicate diamond in her right nostril.

"Are you okay?" she asked, raising one eyebrow at me. She searched my face, probably horrified by my goth-like makeup and flyaway ponytail.

"Yeah, just haven't slept," I admitted. "I'm investigating two missing people: Lily and Nova Nesbitt. Can ya tell me anything about them? Do ya know the husband, Martin?"

"Well, I know he's a realtor and he goes to work every day at nine in the morning. I don't think he's much of a morning person though," she said, staring over at Martin's door with a frown on her face.

"Why do ya say that?"

"Well, I'm never here at night. I work third shift, so usually he's going to work when I'm coming home. Sometimes, I wait until after he's left before lying down because he stomps around, and I've heard him hit the walls before." She gave me a flat, nervous smile.

"Do ya think he was abusing his wife?" I mashed my teeth together, then winced.

"Well, that's the weird thing. Whenever I see him, he's super nice to me. That wife of his...well, she never comes outside, and a few times I tried to knock and ask to borrow something, eggs or what have you, she closed the door in my face. I know this sounds weird, but sometimes I wondered if it was her over there banging on the walls. Cause she seemed like the mean one."

Ugh. This is getting me nowhere, I thought in frustration.

Circles, and more circles.

"What about the little girl? Did ya ever see her outside?" I pushed.

She shook her head. "Nah, I didn't even know they had a kid. Of course, then again, I'm always sleeping during the day and working at night, so I don't see much anyway. I do remember her being pregnant a long time ago, but then her husband said she lost the baby. It was supposed to be a little boy, I think. He seemed sad about it."

I glanced over at Martin's door, wondering if he was on the other side of it now, listening.

"Did ya see him moving anything out of there recently? Furniture, or a bed, maybe?"

Again, she shook her head. Disappointed, I thanked her, and strolled around the right side of the house, circling around to the front fence line. The rain was picking up, but I didn't mind. My mind was twisting and turning, trying to make sense of all this, as my boot struck the edge of a rock. I stumbled forward, catching myself clumsily on the fence.

I looked back at the rock, instantly recognizing it. There were six of them arranged neatly along the fence line, delicate yellow flowers between each one. Squatting down, I studied the row of rocks. Where are the rest of them?

My finger brushed over fresh soil squares where nearly five more stones were missing. The soil where they'd previously sat was darker, fresher than the dirt surrounding the other stones.

This is where those strange stones in Nova's bag came from. But why? Why would she bring these stones with her? She barely brought any clothes, but she thought to bring along garden décor? It didn't seem likely.

Carefully, I wedged one of the stones out of its place and was surprised to discover it was quite heavy. Did Martin bring them along to use as a weapon when he followed them to West Virginia?

Roland and Mike were standing on the sidewalk, looking like two drowned rats.

"There's an umbrella in my cruiser," I told them, peeking through the fence. I filled them in on the stones. "Do you guys mind taking some photographs of where the stones were removed? And we also need to bag up the others to make sure they are, in fact, the same."

Roland rolled his eyes at me, but Mike nodded. "Will do."

I crossed the street to Martin's truck, where a guy around my age, with full-sleeve tattoos on his arms, stared back at me from the driver's side. I noticed he was wearing gloves.

"Hi. Who are you?"

"Max. Chad was supposed to tell you I was coming. I handle most of the forensics in Granton and Mount Juliet. He sent me over to process the truck."

I thought about all those missed calls. What else did Chad want to tell me? Hopefully, he had found more at the cabin.

"Any blood inside?" I asked.

Max shook his head. "Nothing yet. Most of the stains in here look like they came from food or drinks."

I pointed in the back seat. "Those shoes might be the only link we have between our suspect and the missing child. They need to be bagged and tagged asap." The two orange sneakers were still lying on the back floorboard, glittering despite the cloud-covered sun.

"Can you guys handle this for a while?" I shouted over to Mike and Roland. They were squatting in the same spot I was earlier, examining the stones from the garden.

"Why? Where you off to?" Roland asked.

"I'm going to go talk to Nova's family. Try to corroborate her story and get some more info on Martin Nesbitt from their perspective."

I ducked my head inside my jacket as I crossed the street and climbed in behind the wheel of my cruiser. I glanced up one last time at the turn-of-the-century apartment building that Nova used to call her home. "Where the hell are you, Nova?" I asked, digging my cell phone out of my pocket.

I knew I should probably call my boss first, but I dialed mom instead.

"There you are! I've been worried sick," she huffed on the other end of the line.

"I'm totally fine, mom. Sorry to worry you. I got in so late last night that I didn't want to wake you up with my call." I pressed my thumbs to my temples, massaging. I really have to get a mouth guard, I thought, drearily.

"Have you seen him yet?"

"Seen who?" I opened my eyes and stared down at the paper Martin had given me, with Nova's dad and sister's numbers on it. I really needed to get in contact with them asap.

"The asshole ex, that's who! Did you lock him up yet?" my mother asked.

"No, but we did talk to him. He's been less than helpful, to say the least. Claims he doesn't even have a daughter. I was expecting him to say a wide variety of things when we confronted him, but not that. I'm going to talk with her other family members now. Can I c—?"

"I heard there were cadaver dogs at the Appleton Farm," mom cut me off before I could hang up the phone.

"Really?" Quietly, I cursed myself for not calling Sergeant DelGrande first. If they found a body or some other important piece of evidence, I needed to know that now. "I gotta go, mom. Need to call my boss."

"I heard they didn't find anything, though."

I sighed, loudly.

"Listen. I got to go. I'll call you tonight."

"Of course. But when are you c—?" I hung up before she could finish.

I didn't get an answer when I called Rita or Reginald, but I knew where they lived so I decided to drive on over. I tried to call sarge on my Bluetooth as I merged onto the expressway, but like the others, he didn't answer.

The setting sun glared harshly in my eyes, making me sleepy, and making my head pound harder. I turned the radio up to distract me and drove to the small town of Tellico Plains.

With the way my luck was going with this case, I expected to find no one home. But when I parked at the curb in front of a cottage-like A-frame house, I saw a man and woman carrying groceries inside. Even from a distance, I knew the man must be Nova's father. He had the same blue-black hair and rawboned shape.

"Mr. McKinley?"

The handsome man nearly dropped his bags when he saw me. "Oh no. Did something happen to Nova?"

\*\*\*

"There was an incident," Nova's father, Reginald, said, taking a small sip of coffee. Nova's half-sister, Rita, was seated across from me next to her dad. Unlike Nova, she was heavier, with soft blonde curls and green eyes flaked with gold.

Reginald offered me some coffee but out of habit, I'd turned it down. Now, as I stared at the bubbly black liquid they were drinking, I wished I had some caffeine in my system.

"What happened?" I asked, gently. Did they know where Nova was? Did they get into some sort of disagreement with her?

"He seemed great, and then…he just didn't. Martin…I'm talking about Martin. You see, he told Nova that her sister and aunt said things at their wedding, terrible things. But the truth is, they didn't. They were shocked when I asked them about it. I don't understand why someone would lie about something like that. He had no reason, he wasn't provoked…we've always been kind to him," he explained.

"When was the last time you saw your daughter?"

Reginald pursed his lips. They were shaped like a tiny pink Christmas bow. "She stopped by one day last year. I'd been asking and asking for her to come, and finally she gave in and came. But she didn't stay long. Martin kept calling her phone. That man is insecure and controlling. Do you think he did something to my daughter?"

"I don't know, sir, but I'm trying to find that out."

"If she left Martin, I don't know where she'd go. Rita hasn't seen her either." He jabbed a thumb at his daughter and she nodded, staring into her coffee cup.

"And if any other family had been in contact with Nova, they would have told me. The truth is that she has been distant for years now. At first, I blamed her. I thought she was so swept up in her feelings for a man that she'd forgotten about where she came from. But I wasn't always a good father to Nova. I was a raging alcoholic for at least half of her life. I would take it back if I could, but I can't. Over time, I've come to accept the truth."

"And what truth is that, sir?" I asked, leaning forward.

"She grew up with an abusive father and now she is a victim of domestic violence. They say it's a cycle, and I guess that's true. If she left Martin, then she would have come to one of us. She would have had to, because she doesn't have anyone else. Martin made sure of that. I've never even been to their house; can you believe that? The fact that she hasn't called or turned up tells me something that I don't want to believe but that I know to be true: my daughter is probably dead. If she wasn't, we would have heard from her by now."

My heart cracked and split apart for this man. He was trying to act strong, but I could tell that he was like a dam on the verge of bursting open.

"I hope that's not the case, but I promise, I'll do everything in my power to find her. I'm also searching for Lily." I leaned in even further. I studied Reginald's face first, then Rita's.

"Who is Lily?" Reginald asked, taking a slow sip of coffee, his face smooth as glass.

He doesn't know...he really doesn't know he has a granddaughter, I realized. I leaned back in the creaky chair, stunned.

"I met with Nova on a separate occasion, before she disappeared. She reported that her daughter was missing. Lily is your granddaughter, sir."

Reginald's cup of coffee slipped from his hands and shattered on the tile floor at his feet. There goes the dam, I thought, stonily.

# CHAPTER TWENTY-FOUR

*The Neighbor*

## CLARA

"I need to ask you a few questions. May I come inside?"

I imagined myself saying 'no' then closing the door in his face.

"Of course, Sam." I stepped back and gestured for him to come inside. "Would you like some coffee? Water, maybe? It's hot out there, I know." I led the way into the kitchen.

My dining room table was tiny. At most, it could seat four, and right now the leaf was down and there were only two chairs. I'd forgotten to take the trash out today and I realized it had a smell.

"Water would be great," Sergeant Sam said, taking the seat closest to the trash can, his nose twitching as he sat down.

After I got his water, I took the seat across from him, forcing myself to breathe slowly. Right away, I noticed how sweaty he looked, and stressed.

Maybe he's stressed because he knows I killed his friend. He's about to tell me they found Andy's decaying corpse, I thought,

126

desperately. Without asking if he minded, I pulled out my pack of Camels and lit one.

If my smoking bothered him, he didn't let on.

"The dogs were too wound up out there. We couldn't keep them away from your side of the land. Especially the barn. I'm sorry, Clara."

Here it comes, I thought. But why hasn't he arrested me yet?

"We had to contain the search to the inside of the cabin for the time being. They didn't cause too much of a ruckus on your side, I promise."

My body shook with relief. If it was anyone else searching my land, they probably would have found the body. But Sam and I went way back; we'd known each other for years.

"Right now, they're spraying a chemical called luminol inside the cabin. It will glow blue in the presence of blood."

Images of that rusty red stain on the floor sprung into my mind, as I took a deep drag. "But don't you already know there's blood?" I said, coughing forcefully. I stubbed the cig out, disgusted with myself for smoking the whole thing so fast.

Sam frowned. "We took some samples already. But sometimes, we can see more if the perpetrator has cleaned up the scene. Sometimes, we can even see the manner of death."

"Really?"

"Really," he said, still looking grim. The butt was still smoking in the ashtray. Sam stubbed at it for me, staring into the murky ashtray as though it held the answers to my tenant's disappearance. "I need to ask you a few questions, Clara."

"Sure. Of course." I was smiling, despite myself, so relieved they hadn't uncovered my deep, dark secret. *Yet.*

"I'd like you to look at this picture and see if this is the truck you saw?" Sergeant Sam pushed his cell phone across the table toward me. It was a picture taken of a small, black pick-up.

I stared at the picture, trying to keep myself composed. "Where did you see this truck?" I asked, my voice sounding steadier than it felt.

"It's about a quarter of a mile from here, parked in that dirt turnabout near Widow's Curve." That's not what it was actually called, but everyone in Northfolk knew where Widow's Curve was. It was only a ten-minute walk from here.

"Anyone inside the truck?" I asked, the picture turning blurry as I focused too hard.

"No. It was abandoned there. No license plates, nothing. I think this might be the truck you saw parked in front of Nova's cabin on the night she went missing."

I cleared my throat, looking over at my pack of cigs wistfully. I wasn't wondering if I'd seen the truck before because I already knew that I had.

"No, I don't think so. The truck I saw looked larger. Higher up from the ground."

"But you said it was dark. Hard to tell color and size from all the way across the field…"

"Yeah. Maybe," I agreed. Why was that truck parked near Widow's Curve? It wasn't supposed to be there.

My stomach filled with dread. This whole time, I'd been worried about them finding Andy's body, when all along, I had bigger things to be concerned about.

"You okay? You looked peaked," Sam said.

"Fine. This whole thing has sucked the life out of me. I'm worried about my tenant and her little girl. Don't want that husband of hers turning up here again. You think I'm in danger?"

Sam shook his head. "No, I don't. But I can have one of my officers keep an eye out for you tonight. To be honest, I'm not totally convinced that the husband did this. The details are more complicated…I shouldn't be telling you this, but Martin Nesbitt's truck is parked right now nearly twelve hours away. We're searching through it. I can't help wondering if it's just a coincidence, the two trucks…"

"You said there were other things you wanted to ask me," I said, eager to be alone and get my thoughts straight. I needed a cigarette. And I needed this talk to be over with.

"I wanted to ask you about this, too." Sam bent down, lifting up a clear plastic bag. He'd carried it in under his armpit, but I hadn't noticed what was inside. Now, he sat its contents on the table and looked at me.

It was an ugly stuffed rabbit with button eyes. I'd seen it, and many like it, a thousand times before.

"When Officer James told me that they found a stuffed rabbit in the child's bed, I didn't think anything of it. But then today, I saw it in the evidence locker. I recognized it immediately—didn't Andy used to make these?"

I nodded, solemnly. Andy was obsessed with that old sewing machine of his. Besides drinking, it was the only thing that he ever seemed to commit to. Why he chose to make creepy stuffed toys was beyond me. The girls always hated having them in their room. Eventually, I shoved them all into a plastic bag. Like the other unused items in the basement, the bag of bunnies was sitting in a corner. Collecting dust, just like me.

"Any idea why one of Andy's stuffed rabbits would be found in the bed of a missing child?" Sam asked.

I cleared my throat, nodding again. "It was me. I'm the one who put it there," I admitted.

# CHAPTER TWENTY-FIVE

*The Cop*

## ELLIE

My mind was reeling as I pulled into the Granton police station. It was a two-story brick building, a newer, more modern version of our station back home. I still couldn't reach Sergeant DelGrande, but I had a couple texts from Chad. I parked the cruiser, unhooked my seatbelt and thumbed through his message:

**Chad: There were cadaver dogs at the cabin today. They reacted slightly near the blood stain, but it was a minor reaction according to the dogs' owner. I don't know how to interpret that. We couldn't search much outside the residence, though, because the woman next door has a dead kid buried over there. Sorry if that sounds callous, I'm just in a mood today. There was a small hole, just a couple feet deep, that looked freshly dug. But no body and no blood. That hole could have been dug up by coyotes or coons. We're getting ready to spray luminol. Maybe that will tell us something. Will you call me tonight? I'd like to discuss the results with you. Also, the teeth you found: there were strange markings (striations) on them. Did Nova**

sew? **Sometimes dressmakers and tailors hold needles in their teeth while sewing. I'm not sure if that helps you at all, but I found it interesting.**

That *was* interesting, although Nova didn't strike me as the sewing type.

She also didn't strike me as the type to batter and strangle someone, or lie about having children, but I was about to walk into the Granton police station and ask for a copy of the incident report from when she got arrested. I tried sarge one last time, with no luck, then texted Chad back about the stones we'd found and Martin's total denial of his daughter's existence.

I was about to march inside the station to obtain Nova's arrest report when my phone rang. Hoping it was Sergeant DelGrande, I stared down at the unknown number.

"Officer James speaking."

"Hi. Ms. James? It's…it's Rita Clause, Nova's sister. We just met at dad's," said a meek voice on the other line.

"Yes, of course. What can I do for you, Rita?"

The young woman cleared her throat, then said, "I didn't want to say this in front of my dad, but I knew about Lily."

My breath clenched in my chest. I breathed out heavily, through pursed lips. *Thank goodness.*

"Why is Martin denying her existence then, and why didn't your sister tell your dad about his granddaughter?"

"Martin is an asshole, but what he said was true. My sister was pregnant. I saw her. I took her to a few of her appointments. But she lost the baby. She wanted to wait before she told everyone, and then when she miscarried, she never did. It was so painful for her."

My heart fell, and I smacked my hands on the steering wheel. "I already know about the baby, but according to Martin and her neighbor, the child she was carrying was a boy. Are you saying that your sister made it all up? That she called us out there to report a child missing that doesn't even exist?"

"I-I don't know…maybe she was so stressed out over Martin. I never learned the baby's sex…I just know she lost it. That's the only baby I know of. My sister liked to drink sometimes. Are you sure she wasn't drunk and confused?"

I remembered the smell emitting from Nova on the first morning we met. Was it mouthwash or alcohol I smelled? And even if she was drunk…I still couldn't imagine being so intoxicated that I thought my miscarried child was still alive. But…I'd never lost a child. Who could really know what her mindset was? Perhaps she is mentally ill, I considered, glumly.

I asked Rita a few more questions about Nova's history. She admitted that her sister was anxious and depressed sometimes, but no mental disorders had ever been diagnosed by a doctor.

"Thank you, Rita," I said, slamming the phone shut. Circles, and more circles.

I forced myself out of my cruiser and strolled inside the Granton police department. I thought for sure they'd give me trouble, but the place was quiet as a tomb, well, except for the gum-popping teenager working the desk. She was probably in her twenties, but with her freckled cheeks and braces, and that annoying gum, she seemed much younger. I asked for a copy of Nova's arrest report and she asked me for nothing in return, not a flash of my badge or even an ID.

"Thanks," I said, collecting the thick stack of pages that I hoped would give me some insight into Nova Nesbitt.

\*\*\*

Air conditioning pumped from the vents in my hotel room. Despite the unusual humidity outside, I was freezing from the rain. I peeled out of my uniform and tossed it in a corner of the room. One nice thing about being here instead of mom's, was that I didn't have to worry about being neat.

I couldn't stop thinking about the cabin and wishing I was

back in Northfolk. I felt like I owed it to Nova to be there, and there was still so much more work to do. I was convinced that Martin was guilty, but still, they say that most violent crimes occur near your home. All these worried travelers and phobic fears about foreigners, all the while the real danger is probably lurking in your own backyard...

But Northfolk wasn't Nova's home, Granton was, I reminded myself. If something happened to her, then I was probably in the right place because this town was where she lived and breathed...

Please still be breathing, Nova, I silently prayed.

Despite her sister and Martin's reports about the child, I still couldn't believe that Martin was innocent. Nova had been so scared...so convincing...

I took my phone and dialed the station in Northfolk. Everyone should be out working the case, I thought. But I was hoping to catch someone who wasn't down at the scene.

"Northfolk Police Department." I instantly recognized Officer Freis's burly voice. He was one of our newest officers. He'd transferred to our unit from St. Paul last year. I'd had this tiny glimmer of hope that we might connect, both being relatively young, and new to the force. But unfortunately, he'd quickly fallen in line with Roland and the other guys after hearing about my shooting incident.

"Hey, Freis. It's Officer James. I'm surprised you're still in the office."

"Yeah, well, I have a mountain of paperwork to do from last week."

I rolled my eyes. Before Nova Nesbitt came to town, there was very little going on in Northfolk. What sort of paperwork could he possibly be doing?

"What have you been doing for the Nesbitt case? I'm in Granton, so I'm trying to get an update. I already talked to Chad via text earlier."

"Well, we've been reviewing CCTV footage from some of the local stores and bars, looking for any suspicious vehicles, or anyone toting around a strange girl with them," he said. I could hear him rustling papers around. He sounded bored.

"Any luck with that?"

"Nada."

"Well, what about local sex offenders?" My head flooded with images and feelings that I never wanted to think or feel again.

"Yep. Been working on that, too." As Freis started listing off nearly a dozen names, I was shocked to learn that we had so many registered sex offenders in Northfolk and its surrounding counties.

"Can you grab Nichols and maybe you guys can start working through that list, checking out their current status? Make sure they are still living where they're supposed to be living and look inside their houses. Make sure they're not stashing a little girl or a woman there, in other words."

Freis groaned. "Don't we need a warrant to do that?"

"Not if they're on probation or parole. Contact the PO officer on record. They might even go do it for you. You can find all that stuff listed in Shuttel." Shuttel was our central database for local and state-wide criminals. It was also where we could type up our notes and keep them in one place, but most of the guys still insisted on doing it the old way, on paper.

"Wow, that sounds like a whole lot of work. Isn't this your case?" Freis groaned.

"Have you ever noticed the 'work' part in the word 'police work'?" I asked. "There might be a killer in Northfolk, so I think that makes this everyone's problem, don't you?"

I walked over to my hotel window and looked out. Two stories up, my view overlooked the back parking lot. As I stared out at the wet, dark pavement and droopy clouds in the sky, I was hit with a wave of depression. I looked around the lot for signs of life, balancing the phone between my shoulder and ear. Two piercing blue eyes and a teasing smile looked back at me from the sky...Martin Nesbitt's face on a realty advertisement.

I must have made a noise, because Freis asked, "You okay?"

"Peachy." I stared at Martin's over-confident grin. His face was plastered on a billboard; in the distance, it looked huge. It overlooked the highway, larger than life and high above the ground. Martin was one of those high-rise boys who enjoyed hooking up with girls who lived close to the ground, damaged. It was a strange thought, but I couldn't shake it. I was convinced he had to be the one who'd hurt Nova and took her little girl...

"You still there?" Freis asked, sounding tired. I could imagine him hunched over his desk, rubbing sleep from his eyes.

"Call me after you've gone through that list?" I asked him.

"Alright. Talk soon." He clicked off the phone, but it took me a few seconds to realize he was gone. I was still mesmerized by Martin's eyes, the way they seemed to be laughing at me...

With Nova's arrest report in hand, I slithered beneath the hotel sheets and the thick creamy comforter. Nearly forty-eight hours had passed since I last slept. My thoughts were heady and strange, my head and jaw thudding as I leaned against the soft feather pillows in the bed.

I was waiting to hear back from my boss and Roland and Mike for an update on their end. There had to be *something,* some tiny detail would do, anything to crack this case wide open. So far, all I had was a missing child that didn't seem to exist and a slimy husband that gave me the creeps.

I checked my phone for missed calls one more time, then set it on the hotel nightstand. Sinking deeper in the sheets, I started reading the first page of Nova's arrest report. *Domestic Battery, Criminal Confinement and Strangulation.* Some pretty serious charges.

My eyes grew heavy and warm as I scanned through the next three pages. I needed to sleep soon. I wouldn't be able to do any good policework until I got some rest.

I put the arrest report on the nightstand next to my phone and flipped the lamp beside the bed out. Closing my eyes, I tried to imagine that day and what might have really happened. Police reports are so formal and concise; they rarely depict the whole story.

According to the report, police were called to the scene of a domestic disturbance at the Nesbitts' six months ago. They'd received a distress call from Martin Nesbitt. When they arrived, he met them on the porch. Bruised and bleeding, there were distinctive finger print marks circling Martin's neck. *She's lost it, really fucking lost it this time*, he told them. Supposedly, he called them out of fear—his wife, Nova Nesbitt, threatened to kill him if he tried to leave. When asked what provoked the initial argument, Martin admitted that he was a "piece of shit", and that his wife had found images and messages on his phone that revealed he was having an affair. *I shouldn't have called the police, I just got scared she might really kill me.* He begged them not to arrest her, but they did anyway. She was inside, tucked between the toilet tank and sink, when they went inside the apartment. She didn't have a scratch on her. When they asked her why she did it, she just shrugged. She never made a statement, not even after she got arrested, and for the next forty-eight hours, she sat in a holding cell before Martin bailed her out. She went to court a few months later and in open court, Martin stood and pleaded with the judge to drop the charges. The only words Nova ever spoke were 'not guilty'. The judge went easy on her, only assigning one hundred hours of community service.

It was a pretty typical story of domestic abuse, except for the fact that the victim was male in this case. It wasn't unheard of, just less common. Often, the victims dropped the charges after their abuser went to jail, so that part wasn't surprising either.

I tried to imagine Nova, such a wispy, nervous woman, with her hands around Martin's neck. He was a muscular, athletic man, and I was having trouble picturing it. But that was unfair. Just because he's a man doesn't mean he couldn't be a victim of domestic violence. I knew that. My training made *sure* I knew that. But still, he seemed so cocky and arrogant when I was alone with him. I couldn't wrap my brain around this story. A picture was being painted of a crazy woman who told lies. But that's the same thing all of the officers said about Mandy Clark. *She was hard to handle. She drove him to drink. He wasn't really abusive.* Officer Ezra Clark was local, and his wife wasn't. A good old boy who played football in high school, served in the military, and climbed the respected ranks in the police force. His wife was painted as the needy, dramatic one. And when I shot him to protect her and myself, it was like I'd murdered a hero.

I refuse to just accept these stories about Nova being unstable, until I find out where she is and can talk to her myself, I decided.

Closing my eyes, I reviewed the details of the case in my mind until my thoughts turned murky and weird. Sharp, plastic teeth and mangy claws. Big black button-eyes transforming into sunless, shimmery, black puddles that sucked up little girls and ate them alive…

# CHAPTER TWENTY-SIX

**2 years earlier**

*The Mother*

**NOVA**

When I became a mother, nothing changed, much to my disappointment. It was silly of me, thinking things would be different. Not just Martin, but *life*. I thought things might look different somehow, like looking through a new pair of lenses; I thought the world would make either more or less sense; I thought I'd feel like a grown-up. Like a real woman.

But the trees on Meadow Lane still looked the same. The sidewalks are still filled with cracks. *Step on a crack and break your mother's back*, that's what my half-sister Rita and I used to say as we skipped and hopped over fissures in sidewalks when we were little. Since our mothers weren't around, we didn't care if we cursed them or not.

Mailboxes on Meadow Lane all looked the same. Houses loomed like old ghosts and the walls of my apartment with Martin still closed in on me. *Sometimes I don't know if it's the walls, really, or if it's my own skin that's too itchy, too narrow, too tight…*

Lily was tiny and flimsy. She cried, she cooed, and I was terrified to be her mother. I tried to keep her quiet all the time, so as not to upset Martin, but sometimes that wasn't always possible. Other women said, '*Don't worry. When she gets here, you'll be a natural*'. Lies. All lies.

*I'm still the same woman I was before I gave birth to my daughter. Still that same girl from ten years ago, retainer sliding around her teeth and clumsy paws for hands. I'm still me, but I'm not me. And when I look in the mirror, I wonder: where did I go? It's like there are all these versions of me walking around town: the unwanted child, the gawky teen, the free-spirited adult, the abused wife, the inexperienced mother…and none of them are who I want to be, not really. There's me and then there's the reflection of me—these are two very different things.*

Today was my last day of my community service down at the soup kitchen. I rarely left the house anymore, unless it was for my "punishment" the court assigned. *I say "punishment" but it feels like a gift, getting out of the house and away from Martin's watchful eyes and a break from Lily's beggary.*

As I parked at the curb in front of 609 Meadow Lane, I was relieved not to see Martin's truck. I let myself inside the apartment and set my purse on the kitchen counter. I could hear Lily's bubbly laughter, sweet and melodic, floating down the hall from her bedroom. The door was closed and when I pushed it open, my face broke out into a smile. My eyes tickled with tears, the kind of tears that spring up and catch you by surprise. Lily was sitting in the middle of her bedroom floor playing patty cake with Rachel. They both looked up at me and smiled.

"Mommy's home," Rachel squealed, in that childlike, singsongy voice that all adults tend to use when they're in the presence of cute, chubby-faced babies.

"How was it?" she asked, standing up and lifting Lily from the floor. She passed her to me and I squeezed her tight, sucking in her sweet baby smells of lotion and spoiled milk.

"Went f-fine. I'll sort of m-miss helping out d-down there. Does that s-sound crazy?"

Rachel stroked the soft little curls around Lily's neck. "No, of course not. It's nice to get out, Nova. You should do it more often. And just because you're not assigned there anymore, doesn't mean you can't ask to volunteer on your own." Strangely, the idea had never crossed my mind. Probably because Martin would never agree to it. I was lucky enough to be allowed to have Rachel over as a babysitter on my community service days.

I nodded, my eyes glazing over as I stared at the tightly drawn blinds in Lily's room. She rarely saw the sun and I almost wished I could have taken her down to the soup kitchen with me. She would have enjoyed the sights and the smells, and the kind people, who were just so happy to receive a hot meal.

"M-Martin isn't home yet," I said, more to myself than to Rachel.

I could feel her staring, her eyes burning holes in the side of my face. "We're alone for once," she spoke, softly.

I snapped out of my daze. Lily was wiggling around in my arms, eager to run around on the floor. I eased her down, the movement still awkward and scary for me even though she wasn't tiny anymore, and she quickly raced across the carpet toward her basket of toys.

"What d-do you m-mean by that?"

"I just mean, he's always here. That's all. I'm always happy to come watch Lily for you, for any reason. Even if you just want to take a walk, or sleep."

"Thank you, Rachel. I appreciate all your h-help. With watching after Lily, and...my pr-pregnancy with M-Matthew."

"How are you feeling? Would you like me to give you a check-up sometime soon? You're way overdue for one." This wasn't the first time we'd had this conversation. Besides the secret ultrasound when she determined Lily's sex, she hadn't examined me.

"I just wish you would have let me help more…" she said, reaching out and pulling me in for a hug, surprising me. She'd never touched me unless she was examining me, so it was unexpected and shockingly pleasant. "Listen," she said, pulling back and squeezing my shoulders gently, "before he gets back, I wanted to give you this."

"What i-is it?" I watched her take out a small card from her right jeans pocket.

"It's a knitting club. I think it would be good for you, Nova."

"Oh." Dumbfounded, I accepted the card and turned it over and back. It was white and nondescript, with a website address in the center. Knitting tips dot com. I'd never knitted a single thing in my life. Home Ec was still required when I went to school and for the second half we learned about sewing. I preferred the cooking and the eating part of the semester because my hands were too shaky to hold the fabric straight. My teacher, Miss Langley, told me I was one of the worst she'd ever seen. I could have told Rachel this, but I didn't have the heart.

But she must have seen the confused look on my face as I thanked her and set the card on Lily's dresser, because she said, "You should check it out. It's not at all what you think. It could be therapeutic for you. Promise me you'll at least look at the website?"

I wanted to say, *yes, of course*, but I couldn't lie. "Rachel, our internet here is w-wonky. I've g-given up on trying to get it to w-work for a w-while now. But if it ever g-gets straightened out, I will d-definitely look it up."

"Your husband's internet seems to work just fine. I see him posting pics about his realty accomplishments on Facebook and Instagram all the time," she snapped. She looked red and flustered all of a sudden.

"He d-does?" This was news to me, but it didn't really surprise me.

Rachel grabbed my hand and squeezed it just as I heard Martin's key turning in the lock. My body instantly tensed up, the way it always did when Martin came through the door. I never knew what to expect as my body jarred in anticipation.

"It's not just for knitting," Rachel breathed, her words quiet as wind whistling through a seashell. Then she said, louder now, "Well, good luck with everything, Nova. If you guys need me in the future, please don't hesitate to call."

I nodded, still shaken and nervous for some reason, then I walked over to where Lily was sitting on the floor. She was gnawing on one of her rubber duckies and when I tried to dislodge it from her tiny grasp, she screamed. Scooping her up, I held her to my chest and rocked her forward and back in my arms. Anything to make her stop crying before Martin came in the room. Lily was usually a quiet baby, but now that she was walking and starting to talk some, it was getting harder to control her bursts of emotion. But still, I had better luck managing her emotions than I did managing Martin's, a full-grown man.

I could hear him talking to Rachel in the kitchen. I couldn't make out all the words, but I thought I heard Rachel ask, "Will you help her download this knitting app?" and something about wanting to teach me how to make baby booties and scarves.

# CHAPTER TWENTY-SEVEN

## *The Neighbor*

### CLARA

Two nights in a row, I visited my dead husband. Insects buzzed in the field surrounding the barn, their chirps and cries either a warning or an accusation.

Online, I'd read about the four stages of decomposition. Andy was in stage three—active decay. Besides his hair, bones, and some cartilage, most of what used to be my bastard husband was rotting away. The unusually hot weather was speeding up the process, too.

I couldn't help thinking about my baby girl, too, lying in the hard, cold ground by the barn, consumed by darkness and bugs. Oh, how she hated the dark...by now, Annie's body had probably skeletonized. The soft baby fat on her cheeks...and the lips I used to kiss every night were gone.

"What am I going to do?" I asked, looking at my husband's corpse. In life, he rarely knew the answers or did anything to make my life easier, so I don't know why I was asking now.

I'd been down here a dozen times since the incident. It still

143

didn't seem real—again and again, I saw myself, as though I were floating outside my own body, as I hit him over the head with the shovel.

I needed to move his body or find a way to destroy it. But now that he was down here in this hidden cellar, I couldn't see a way of getting him back up the hole. I'd used the wheel barrow to lift his body and dump it down through the hole, but now... *now*...I was in quite a predicament.

The smell was atrocious. My stomach heaved, and I couldn't shake the thought that he could hear me somehow. Or was his spirit somewhere in here with me, in the barn, waiting to haunt me forever...

When I was little, one of my sisters had died. It wasn't considered a violent death, but it had felt pretty violent to me. A fever had taken over, so high and consuming, that it broiled her tiny body from the inside out. For years, I waited for her ghost to crawl in bed beside me at night, the way she used to when she was alive. Our spindly legs intertwined, secrets shared between the sheets...But she never came, and as I grew older, I realized I was silly for hoping she would, and for believing in ghosts in the first place. I had another sister who lived, but I could never fill that hole in my heart. It's strange how when you're little, you want to believe in everything. As you grow older, all those beliefs scatter away and disperse, only to return again after you've lived long enough to know that anything is possible.

The farm was full of ghosts now...my grandparents, mama, daddy, sis, and now my own husband and child. Even Krissy, who was still alive, haunted me sometimes. I imagined the younger version of her, racing through tall rows of corn, shouting for me to catch her if I could...

"Goodbye," I said to Andy, stiffly. Then I climbed the crooked rungs of the ladder and closed the barn up tight behind me.

Today, I'd been lucky. I'd been so sure the cops would find

Andy. If it wasn't for Officer DelGrande being so respectful of my daughter's death, they most certainly would have.

Maybe there was a small part of me that wished they had. At least then they'd know how to deal with his body. And at least I'd finally be punished for what I did. Because as monstrous as my actions were, that wasn't who I really was...*I'm not a killer, but I have killed...*

I'd considered chopping up his body and carrying it up in pieces. But just the thought alone made me want to vomit...*I can't...*

According to my google search, luminol faded in thirty minutes or so. But as I approached the smoky smudge of the cabin, I was wracked by images of black lights and blood-splattered rooms, like something straight out of a horror movie.

It was barely dark, the tight little knots of police personnel finally crumbling apart and leaving my property, one vehicle at a time. The moon kissed the clouds as I slipped through the shadowy trees past the cabin. A few yards away inside the farm-house, tucked away in my drawer, were my smokes. I yearned for a cigarette. I tasted smoke in my lungs.

I cut through a gap between two trees and emerged on the main road that ran in front of the farm. Even though darkness had fallen, Northfolk still had that seven o'clock dinner hush hanging in the air. I followed the twisted, newly-paved road up a steep incline and then around two sharp curves, watching care-fully for blind-curve speedsters, or anyone who might wonder what I was up to.

I didn't expect the truck to still be there. After Sam told me about it, I'd assumed they'd already had it towed to the station to be searched. But there it sat in the dirt roundabout that truckers and cars used if they couldn't slow themselves down fast enough while winding around Widow's Curve.

The story behind how it got its name went something like this: a man and a woman fell in love and planned to be married.

Nobody remembers their actual names. On the day of the ceremony, she was with her family getting ready and he was doing the same with his own. They were both so worried about impressing the other, that they were both running late for the ceremony. He got to the chapel first and when he didn't see her, he panicked and turned around, driving to her sister's house. She was rushing to get to the church and he was rushing to get to her, and as they both met at the sharp curl of the curve, they slammed into each other head on. His car toppled over the side of the mountain. When she got out of her own car, she dragged herself to the edge of the drop-off. Distraught over her lost love, she climbed back into her car and drove straight off the mountain to join him.

I never really believed that story. Or that the curve was cursed. But suddenly, I was having my doubts. Looking around, I slowly approached the driver's side of the truck. Both doors were locked tight. I cupped my hands around my face. Peeked in through the driver's side window.

This didn't seem right. This truck had no business being in this spot.

Hands quivering, my urge to smoke overwhelming, I took my cell phone out of my back pocket. I didn't want to call, but now there was no other choice. Nothing about this made sense.

The phone rang once, then went to voicemail. *Damn.*

My voice was shaking as I left a short message: "What the hell is your truck doing here?"

# CHAPTER TWENTY-EIGHT

*The Cop*

## ELLIE

"Your message said you know how the bunny got there?" my voice cracked. I was sitting in a McDonald's parking lot with the windows rolled down in my cruiser, rubbing my stiff jaw and rotating my neck in pointless circles.

"It was Clara Appleton. I talked to her today," Sergeant DelGrande explained. It sounded like he was driving, wind blowing and low music whistling in the background. I thought I heard the raspy lyrics of Bonnie Raitt.

"What?!" I cranked my driver's window back up and leaned forward in my seat.

"Clara's husband used to make stuffed toys. I showed it to her and she confirmed that it was one of his. I guess she put it there before they moved in. She knew a little girl was coming and thought she might like the toy."

"Hmmm. I don't know how anyone could like that creepy little thing. So, what else did ya find? What'd the luminol show?"

"Well, that's what's bothering me. There's no spatter or areas that appear to have been cleaned up. The only thing we can tell is that someone smeared that blood around on the floor. Those empty containers with the rusted-out bottoms, the ones we found in the bag? The only blood we can get off them is bovine, too. It looks like someone dumped containers of cow blood on the floor, then smeared it around. The only trace of a human there is those teeth."

"So, you think she, or someone else, staged the scene then?" I sighed.

"That's how it looks to me. She was running from her husband. Maybe she wanted him, and everyone else, to think she was dead," Sergeant DelGrande suggested.

"But, then why call us in the day before and tell us her daughter went missing? What would be her motivation there?"

"No idea. The whole situation is strange," Sergeant DelGrande agreed. "Maybe she wanted to distract us while she ran out of town."

"Kind of hard to get the hell out of dodge without your car," I said, picturing the Celica parked in the driveway.

"That's true. But, maybe she had a boyfriend, or a friend, who picked her up."

"Clara Appleton described a truck that matches Martin's, so I definitely think he was involved. Unless she's changed her story about what she saw?"

"No, she hasn't. But we did find an abandoned truck less than a quarter mile away. No license plates on it. I'm trying to get the Vin number off it now, but it looks like someone tried to rub it off. Got some guys working on it now, though, so we should know pretty soon who it's registered to," he said.

"Does it meet the description Clara gave?"

"Black, two-door, pick-up. I showed her a picture. She didn't recognize it but said it could be the one. It doesn't belong to anyone in Northfolk, at least it doesn't appear to. So, Mr. Nesbitt's truck might never have left Granton, far as we know now," Sam explained.

Closing my eyes, I leaned my head against the seat. Nothing about this case made sense. One minute, Martin Nesbitt seemed guilty as sin and the next minute there was some other random vehicle to throw in the mix.

"What about Clara Appleton's house and outbuildings? Anything suspect there?" I asked, massaging my temples.

"No, of course not. Clara's a good woman and she's being as helpful as possible," Sam said, a slight edge to his voice.

"I know you guys are friends, but we have to dig deeper, sarge. What about her husband? She said he left her for another woman. I'd like to talk to him, just to verify his current whereabouts." I expected Sam to put up a fight on that, too, but he gave me his name: Andy Appleton.

"She said he was in Florida with his mistress. I don't know the address or phone number there, or her name," sarge said slowly, seemingly lost in thought.

"Well, I'll ask Clara, okay? That way you don't have to. We need to double check that her husband wasn't involved in Nova's disappearance. Can't rule anything out," I pondered.

There was a soft knock on my window and I jerked up in my seat. "Let me call you back, sarge," I said, clicking off my cell phone.

There was a man bent down, staring in at me. He had caramel-colored hair and eyes, and his face looked grim and worrisome.

"What do you want?" I asked through the window.

For as long as I'd been old enough to understand the dangers of being a woman alone in a parked car, I'd refused to roll my windows down for strangers.

But now I was a cop, so I sort of had to. This man could be in trouble, I realized.

Reluctantly, I cracked my window. "What can I do for you, sir?"

"I'm Brad Cummings. Would you like to have lunch?"

Un-fucking-believable. Even in uniform, I couldn't get a man to respect me.

"Sir, I'm a police officer. I'm working, so I'll be dining alone. But thanks." I started to roll my window back up, when he snorted with laughter.

"Sorry. I'm *Detective* Brad Cummings. I'm so used to everyone knowing me around here. I wasn't hitting on you just now, I swear. I saw you parked here and thought maybe we could talk about something during lunch hour."

My cheeks flushed with shame. "Oh, alright. What did ya want to talk about? I was going to hit the drive thru. I'm in town getting information for a case back in Northfolk, West Virginia. I'm leaving town soon."

Cummings's cheerful expression morphed back into its steely mask. "Well, that's exactly what I wanted to talk to you about. I work for the Granton police force and I heard that an officer was down at my precinct today, picking up a police report on one Nova Nesbitt."

"Yep, that's correct." For some reason, I felt like I was about to get scolded. But as he opened his mouth and started talking, I realized that couldn't be further from the truth.

"I need your help. I'm conducting a missing persons investigation that might be linked to yours," he said, his tone deadly serious.

# CHAPTER TWENTY-NINE

**1 year earlier**

*The Mother*

## NOVA

It wasn't until months later that I checked out the knitting site Rachel had recommended. I probably never would have, either, if Martin hadn't come home one day carrying another one of those stupid cards.

"I ran into Rachel Coffey at the supermarket today. She said you haven't returned her calls."

I was sitting on the living room couch, bouncing Lily on my lap. I didn't like watching TV whenever Martin was home, or else he called me lazy. But now that Lily was almost four, she'd taken a hankering to cartoons, especially Doc McStuffins.

"She was my m-midwife once, M-Martin. An oc-ccasional babysitter…We weren't fr-friends. I'm so b-busy around h-here that I r-really don't have time to ch-chat, and that woman likes to t-talk." I was saying what he wanted to hear. The real reason I cut off contact with Rachel was the same reason I lost contact with everyone else. You couldn't maintain friendships when your controlling husband was always around and watching, and Lily really did keep me busy most days. Since Martin was opposed to preschool, I was teaching her things myself. ABCs and 123s, who knew it would be so hard to explain these things to a child? I was a terrible teacher, impatient at times and Lily hated sitting still. She hadn't displayed any signs of a stutter yet, but I wondered if it was only a matter of time…

Martin set his briefcase down in the kitchen and came over to the couch beside us.

"What's that in y-your hand?" I asked, scooting over so he had room to sit down.

"Rachel gave it to me. She really wants you to join her knitting group." He handed a small white card to me.

"I don't knit, Martin. I'm n-not g-good at sewing, you know that."

"But it couldn't hurt to try, could it?" His face softened, and for a moment, I caught a glimpse of the pseudo-Martin, the one he'd murdered years ago when the real one emerged.

"I s-suppose not. But the internet is down again a-and…why do y-you w-want me to learn how to knit?"

"Rachel said it would be good for you, babe. And she said that sometimes knitting little booties and stuff can help put women in a motherly mood." Martin glanced down at my newly flattened tummy then wiggled his brows. I'd worked my ass off getting back in shape and letting my body heal from the traumatic delivery. I'd watched outdated exercise tapes with Lily during the day, slowly repairing my body. The truth was, he probably wanted me to get pregnant again, so I wouldn't feel attractive anymore. He had brought up the idea of having another child last year and had been bugging me about it ever since. Since I didn't have a gynecologist anymore, I'd been unable to refill my birth control pills. Not getting pregnant yet was just me getting lucky.

"Here. I'll download the app on your phone tonight and I'll

make sure the internet is working properly. Tomorrow, you can join this little knitting club. It would be good for you to chat with some other mothers and learn a thing or two about knitting, don't you think? That would really please me."

I nodded, staring straight ahead at the screen. Doc was trying to help a pretty Flamenco dancer named Flora overcome a fear of leaving her box; I'd seen the episode six or seven times now. *I know the feeling, Flora,* I thought. I was scared to live in my little box with Martin, and scared to live out of it, too.

That night, Martin downloaded the app on my phone, as promised. He entered a code for the Apple store—a code he refused to give me—and handed the phone back to me. When Lily went to bed, and Martin fell asleep on the couch, I clicked on the app. *What did Rachel say that day?* It had been so long since we'd had that conversation. *She said that it wasn't really for knitting.* I suspected it was something silly, like an erotic book club or a lingerie site. *I swear if I catch a beating because of this site, I'll kill her myself.*

As soon as I clicked on it, it prompted me to enter a username, password, and promo code. I clicked the "set up a new account" option in small print at the bottom, then laid back on my bed as I waited for it to load. *This is stupid. I don't want to knit. And I don't want to chat with Rachel or her prissy friends. Period.* The only reason I was doing it now was to get Martin off my back.

I had to choose a username and set up a password. I thought for a few moments. I didn't have too many passwords anymore. I didn't have accounts on social media and I stopped checking my email years ago. None of it was worth it with Martin around, questioning my every move and motive.

Finally, I decided on *PrettyPeaches* for my username and my childhood phone number for my password. Within seconds, I was into the site. Eyes wide with fear, I looked over at Martin and then back down at the screen, stunned by what I found there…

# CHAPTER THIRTY

*The Cop*

**ELLIE**

For lunch hour, the rundown dining room in McDonald's was deserted. I sat across from Detective Cummings, unable to touch my fish fillet as he opened a file folder of photos.

"Her husband reported her missing on Saturday, the 19th. She went out for a run in Deer Place Park, and never came home." He pushed a photo across the table to me.

"Who is she?" I asked, staring at a woman with beautiful black hair and bright blue eyes. She looked to be around thirty years old.

"A local woman. Rachel Coffey. Her husband's name is Gil. He's a mess right now."

"Unfortunately, this is not the same woman I'm looking for. But we are investigating Martin Nesbitt. He and his wife live on Meadow Lane and she went missing. Before that, though, she reported her daughter missing. Mr. Nesbitt claims she's crazy and controlling, and that they don't have any children. Why do you think the cases are related, besides the fact that two of your citizens are missing? Is Ms. Coffey connected to Mr. Nesbitt somehow?" I asked, my eyes fluttering back down to the photo.

"I was just over at Gil and Rachel's apartment this morning, checking out her contacts and searching for signs of foul play onsite. I wrote down all the names and addresses I could find in her appointment book. Now, I didn't pay much attention to the actual names, figuring I'd look over them when I got back to the office. But one of the names was a little strange, so it stood out a bit. *Nova.* No last name, no phone number or address. But imagine my surprise when I got back, and my assistant told me there was an out-of-town officer here, asking for an arrest report on someone named Nova Nesbitt and that a warrant had been issued to search her home."

"That can't be a coincidence," I said, soaking my fries in barbeque sauce.

"Exactly." Officer Cummings plucked up a fry. I watched him chew, my stomach twisting in knots, and I told him everything I knew about Nova's case. Was Rachel Coffey the missing link? Was she involved with Nova in some way?

"So, the husband denies having a daughter? What about a birth certificate, some sort of medical history on file?" he pressed.

"That's one of my next steps. I called several local dentists and doctors this morning and she's not a patient there. It's almost like neither mother nor child existed, like he kept them hidden away."

"I don't know Nova Nesbitt. Of course, I don't know everyone in this town, but still. The name doesn't ring a bell. His name, though, the husband's…I'm very familiar with Martin. His face is on billboards and benches, that steely smile advertising his realty business."

"Something about that man gives me the creeps. He seemed so polished and rational when we first spoke, but the moment I was alone with him, his entire demeanor changed. What did you say Rachel did for a living?" I picked up my sandwich and mushed

155

it around in barbecue sauce too. Chewing even the softest bread made my teeth ache.

Officer Cummings smiled. "She's a midwife."

My eyebrows shot up.

"Exactly," he said again. "What are the chances that you got a missing woman and child, and a husband who denies the child exists, at the same time a local midwife goes missing? What if Nova's daughter doesn't exist on paper because Rachel Coffey delivered the baby in her home?"

"But isn't there still paperwork to be filed? You still get a birth certificate for a baby born at home," I wondered aloud.

"Yes, but there are forms to fill out. What if that was never done?"

"It's possible. But we searched his place and didn't find anything, besides a pair of girl's tennis shoes that we suspect Lily had on when he took her." My thoughts drifted back to my conversation with Sergeant DelGrande about the other truck. That still confused me. "Did Rachel Coffey or her husband drive a black pick-up truck?"

Officer Cummings frowned. "I don't think so. They both drive SUVs."

"Any reason to suspect this woman's husband was involved? Gil?" I pressed.

"Well, you never know, but I got the sense that he was absolutely devastated when she went missing. He's called me every couple hours since it happened, wanting constant updates. This connection with the Nesbitts is the first lead I've had so far. What about luminol at Martin's apartment? We used it in Rachel's loft this morning but came up with nothing. It doesn't appear as though she met with foul play there."

"It's worth a shot," I said, knuckling my tray aside. "If you take me to Gil, I'll take you to Martin. Deal?"

He smiled. "Deal."

I followed Officer Cummings's blue Sedan as he pulled out of the McDonald's parking lot. My phone was buzzing in my center console, so I slid my Bluetooth on and answered. I'd been hoping it was the sergeant again, so I could update him, but it was Chad.

"Guess where I am?" he asked, his voice too bubbly for my current mood. I was focused, adrenaline pumping through my veins and my jaw flexing, uncontrollably. I couldn't prove Martin had kidnapped his wife and daughter, but I felt like I was getting closer. Luminol might reveal something, anything, even if it was just a connection to the other kidnapping. And maybe Gil knew Nova Nesbitt and could offer some insight into this woman I'd only met once.

"Are you there?" Chad cut into my thoughts.

"Yes! Sorry. Where are ya?"

"I'm standing in front of your hotel. I'm here to help with the case. I figured you needed someone here and I thought I'd look at those cell phones for you." I could hear the smile in his voice.

"Chad, you're a life saver. But I won't be there for a while. We're heading over to talk to the husband of another missing local woman, and then to the Nesbitt residence to see what we can find using luminol. Want to meet me at the Nesbitts' in an hour or so?" I asked, hoping he'd say yes.

"Who's 'we'?"

"Officer Brad Cummings. A local midwife has gone missing, and she's connected to Nova somehow. I think she might have been Nova's midwife. Maybe the only person who knew about Lily's existence."

"You think Martin killed her to shut her up? If she was the only one who knew about Lily and he's the one that took her, then that's motive," Chad gushed. Suddenly, his chipper demeanor was starting to rub off on me.

"Yes, it is! I just want to find these women and figure out what they're hiding, and why."

"Tell me the address and I'll meet you there in an hour," he said.

I told him where the Nesbitts lived and hung up, just as Officer Cummings turned into a residential neighborhood. He parked at the curb of a rundown, but clean, apartment complex called Fountain Square.

I followed him into the building and up two flights of stairs. An attractive man wearing a running suit answered the door. Despite his neat appearance, his face was a mess. His eyes looked red and dry, and I realized he'd clearly been crying recently.

"Hi, Mr. Coffey. I'm Officer Ellie James. May we come in?"

Gil shot a confused look at Officer Cummings, but then opened the door and let us both in. I quickly explained to him that I was investigating another missing person case, one that may be linked to his wife.

"She didn't discuss her patients with me. She was always very discrete and professional. It frustrated me sometimes...but Martin Nesbitt? I know who he is. In fact..."

"What is it?" Officer Cummings asked, leaning toward him.

"I don't think my wife liked him much. She was always making noises and rolling her eyes when we passed his signs he advertises his business on. I asked her once what she had against the guy, but all she said was: 'He just looks like an asshole to me.'"

Officer Cummings and I exchanged hopeful glances.

"Is it possible that your wife and Nova were friends, and that's why she wasn't crazy about Martin Nesbitt? Could she have possibly been one of your wife's clients? Officer Cummings saw her name in your wife's schedule book," I said.

Gil frowned. "If Nova's name was in her book, then she definitely saw her as a client or met with her for something work-related at some point. Because Rachel kept her close friends' names and numbers stored in her cell phone only."

I looked over at Officer Cummings. He shook his head. "There was nothing in her phone so far about a person named Nova."

Disappointed, I looked around the neat apartment, trying to gain a sense of who Rachel was.

"If your wife delivered a baby in someone's home, would she file the paperwork needed to get a birth certificate?"

Gil nodded. "Absolutely. Rachel loved her clients and always tried to accommodate their individual birth plans and personal needs, but she was a stickler for paperwork and following the law."

"Even if Nova or Martin asked her not to...?"

Gil was staring over my shoulder, his eyes fuzzy. When I glanced over my shoulder, I saw what he was looking at: a wedding photo of himself and the same black-haired beauty in the photo Officer Cummings had shown me.

When I looked back at him, his eyes were focused on me again.

"She wouldn't do that, but...well, there is one way that a child can be born and not require a birth certificate. But it would require the mother giving birth completely on her own, without medical assistance. My wife was familiar with this and explained it to me one night. I think she knew someone who delivered her own baby...maybe that was Nova. But why would they both go missing? Do you think someone kidnapped them? Could Martin Nesbitt be involved...if so, I'll kill him myself!"

Officer Cummings stepped in and reassured Gil, while I thanked him and saw myself out. Back in my cruiser, I left a voicemail for Sergeant DelGrande, updating him on the other missing woman.

\*\*\*

When I pulled up at the Nesbitt residence, I was surprised to see Mike and Roland there.

"Where've you been? Did you forget we were your partners when you left this morning? We had to take an Uber to get over to the lab, and another to get back here," Roland barked.

"I'm sorry, guys." I updated them on Rachel Coffey.

"Any news from the lab yet?" I asked.

Mike shook his head. "Not yet but they're working on it." I gave him the keys to the cruiser, so they could get back and forth from the lab.

I was relieved to see Chad pulling in. He was smiling, his cheeriness contagious. I caught myself smiling despite myself. It felt good, having a co-worker that seemed to trust me and wasn't hung up on the Clark shooting.

Officer Cummings approached us, his mocha hair blowing back in the wind. He was wearing navy blue slacks and a white polo. He took the lead as we knocked on Martin's door. For some reason, I expected him not to be home.

If he's guilty, why hasn't he tried to take off and leave town yet? I wondered.

Maybe he's just that arrogant, I considered. I thought back to our first meeting yesterday. When the other officers were out of the room, his personality seemed to change, and not for the better.

"Hello again, officers!" Martin threw open the door, wearing a cheesy smile that probably looked like the one plastered on his business card. He was shirtless with a wet towel on his head.

"Mr. Nesbitt, I'm Officer Brad Cummings. Granton Police. We need you to step outside for a minute, please, and afterward, we need to talk."

I expected him to put up a fight or ask questions, but he just rolled his eyes and tossed his towel onto the hallway floor. "Suit yourself."

Cummings had a small kit in his hands that looked like a fisherman's tacklebox.

"You ready?" he asked me. I stepped inside the apartment, instantly feeling lighter now that Martin was no longer inside it. That man just had a tension about him, something I couldn't define...

The apartment looked neat and tidy, the same as it had yesterday. Today, without Martin hovering around me, I walked around looking at the few mementos the couple had while Officer Cummings prepared the luminol.

I'd learned about luminol at the academy but had never been involved in a case where it was used. When Sergeant DelGrande had told me they used luminol in the cabin while I wasn't there, I'd been a little disappointed. Today, I was excited to use it for the first time in my career, even under these circumstances...

"So, refresh my memory: we can still see blood, even if it was cleaned up, right?"

"Yes. Even if it's been years since the incident occurred, it will still react with the iron in hemoglobin, which is a protein in our red blood cells," Cummings explained.

"Good. I want to find something that we can use to nail this prick." My eyes slid over the Nesbitts' wedding photo. I zeroed in on a photograph of the couple that had been taken in the living room. It was obvious that Martin had been the one to take the photo because there was a sliver of his right arm in the far-right frame. Nova's smile looked perfect but practiced.

"Is it just me, or is there a funny tint to her face, like she's wearing more makeup on one side?"

Officer Cummings was kneeling down on the floor, unloading a professional-looking camera and spray bottle. He squinted up at the picture on the wall. "Can't tell from here."

"Sort of looks like she was covering up a bruise..." I lamented. Suddenly, I noticed something in the background of the photo

161

beside it. Behind Martin and Nova, I could see the blond wood flooring that lined their living room. There they were—tiny land-mines. A stack of blocks in the corner. Scattered Lego pieces on the floor. And on the window sill, a rubbery doll that might have been a Barbie.

"Bingo." I took the picture down from the wall and slid the picture out of it. It wasn't much, in terms of evidence, but it was something. Something to show that Nova and Martin weren't the only ones living inside this apartment. It was the first actual evidence of a child being inside one of their houses, and it was a relief to see it there.

"What do you think he did with her stuff? The little girl's?" I asked, watching Officer Cummings double-checking the film on the Polaroid camera.

"Not sure. But there's a landfill less than twenty miles from here. Maybe we could look there."

"How can I help you guys?" Chad asked, hands folded neatly behind his back.

"Are you good at taking pictures? This stuff only lasts a half hour. If we do get some sort of result, we'll need to get plenty of shots with this." Officer Cummings held up the camera.

Chad nodded and took the camera, then Officer Cummings handed me the spray bottle.

"Where do you think we should start?" Officer Cummings asked.

"Might as well start in there," I said, pointing toward the living room.

I started spraying the wood floor and walls. "Furniture too?" I asked him.

"Everywhere."

By the time I was done, the entire living room was coated with luminol. Officer Cummings closed the drapes and flipped out the lights, making the apartment as dark as a tomb.

Immediately, parts of the floor glowed blue.

"Bingo," Cummings whispered.

There was blood, blue splatters spread out over five small sections in the living room by the coffee table.

"It's not a ton of blood, but it's still blood," he said. He pointed at a dry spot on the floor "Spray more here."

I sprayed more, creating a skinny blue streak that stopped before the kitchen.

"He attacked her in the living room. Maybe even dragged her toward the kitchen. All the way to the door. It could be Rachel's blood or Nova's…or even Lily's…" Officer Cummings hushed.

"Are you getting pictures of this?" I glanced over at Chad.

His face was whiter than usual. Like me, he was new and young to the force, and probably hadn't seen many scenes like the ones we'd recently encountered.

"Oh yeah." He lifted the camera and started snapping.

Next, I went into the kitchen, hall, and bedroom, but didn't find anything there. The only room left by then was the bathroom. I flipped the bathroom lights out and started spraying. At first, I thought there was nothing, but then I reached the tub.

My eyes widened as the first letter appeared in blue on the wall. I kept spraying until the entire message was revealed. "Hurry, Chad! Get in here," I shout-whispered.

Officer Cummings was the first to pop his head through the door. "My god," he said, looking at the twenty-five-letter message on the wall above the bath tub.

Chad came in behind him and gasped. He snapped photos as the words floated on the back of my tongue, making my mouth water with vomit: MARTIN IS GOING TO KILL US. – NOVA, was written in blood on the wall.

"She wrote that in her own blood. Even while dying, she wanted to make sure he got caught," I said. But did it seem too easy, too obvious…? She obviously wanted to leave this behind for the police to find, but why? Was she murdered here or could she really have staged the whole thing? For the first time, I started to wonder if Sergeant DelGrande was right. Could this all be a decoy?

"Well, now we can at least identify one of his victims. I wish Rachel Coffey had left a message, too," Cummings sighed.

"Let's go arrest him and see what he has to say about this," I said, darting out of the bathroom before they could see my eyes watering.

# CHAPTER THIRTY-ONE

**6 months earlier**

*The Mother*

**NOVA**

When I learned what the site was really for, my face burned with shame.

If I logged in with only my username and password, the site was a normal knitting club that featured members' instructional videos, collages of knitting projects, and page after sunny page of patterns that you could use to knit the scarf of your dreams. But when I used my member code I'd received during registration, it pulled up another version of the site—like the "upside-down" of knitting. There were knitting images and advertisements on the borders, but that's not what the site was for. It was an "online shelter", a means of support for victims of domestic violence. Former survivors helping victims leave their current abusers, or sometimes, they just offered a nonjudgmental ear. There was information about actual, real-life shelters, and with the click of a button, I could join a waiting list for a discrete shelter in my state.

Women supporting women, and there were men too. But not just support. Sometimes they saved each other, too. Like Roberta, for instance. One night, Roberta's husband turned more violent than usual. She sent her mentor a safe word which apparently meant "call police now", and when they got there, she had a gunshot wound. They took her husband to jail and they saved Roberta's life just in time. Now Roberta was one of the mentors and she liked sharing her story.

The first time I learned what the site really was, I felt humiliated, angry and scared. *If Rachel knows, then who else does? Does my family suspect? And, who the hell does she think she is? What if Martin finds out? He'll kill me; he might even kill Rachel.*

I closed the app and it stayed that way for a couple months. Then one day, after Martin screamed at me for letting Lily get up too early and threatened to shut her up himself, I logged back in. I'd told myself that I didn't even remember my "special code". But my fingers remembered as I punched in the letters, and I sat on my bed, staring at the menu screen while Martin slept less than a few inches from me.

There were safeguards in place, like the app would shut itself off if you were idle for longer than sixty seconds, which honestly, was a pain in the ass most of the time. And if you clicked the exclamation point five times, the app would lock you out until you called to restore your account. It was a safe place, or at least it was designed to be.

That first night on the site, and for many nights after, I lurked. I read the other members' posts—some of them had successfully escaped their abusers and some had decided to stay. You could comment on the posts, and I was shocked to see that no one ever posted anything judgmental. Maybe there was an admin who screened the comments for nastiness, but I liked to think the "club" was so tight-knit (pun intended) that we respected each other's decisions and knew, personally, that pushing never helped a woman leave. We were, as corny as it sounded, learning to "stitch" ourselves back together, one thread at a time.

There were articles and resources. Quizzes and lists to help identify signs of abuse. Personal online journals to document incidents and upload photos, if needed.

I found myself clicking on it most afternoons while Lily ate lunch or watched cartoons. I was scared to post anything or make a comment. Scared of leaving some sort of footprint on the world and scared of being judged, even though these women didn't seem like the judge-y type.

I finally filled out my profile some and added a user pic. I even typed out a big long post about my father and Martin, but then I deleted it before I clicked "post". Two days after that, when I logged on, there was a message in my inbox.

I dreaded reading whatever message awaited me, and I put off reading it for hours. But then, finally, I realized it was from one of the members. The name on the account was simply *Al*, with a profile pic like most other profile pics on the site: not a personal photo. It was a stack of books with a rose on top. I'd seen Al a few times before, commenting on others' posts. *What could this person possibly want from me?* Taking a deep breath, I clicked on the message.

**Al: I like your profile pic. Northanger Abbey is one of my favorite Jane Austen novels. There's this line I like: "There is nothing I would not do for those who are really my friends. I have no notion of loving people by halves, it is not my nature."**

I wasn't sure what to say, but it made me smile. A few days later, I responded.

**Me: Jane Austen is great, but lately I've been reading more modern stuff. Have you heard of the *Twilight* series? I thought I'd hate them, but they're really good. Hold on, let me go find one so I can tell you the author's name.**

**Al: !! You don't get out much do you? That series is every-**

where these days! They made them into movies, have you seen them?

My face heated up when I read that response. Martin gave me books, but I couldn't remember the last time I'd gone to a bookstore myself. I didn't know if a book was selling well, or in the "bestseller" section, these days.

**Me: No, I guess I don't get out much, like you said. No, didn't know.**

Al wrote me again, but I logged out. *Even the other members are shocked about how little I get out—how sad is that?*

The next time I signed into the club app, I had three unread messages waiting for me.

**Al: I'm sorry if you thought I was making fun of you. I don't want you to think I was trying to put you down, please don't think that.**

**Al: Hey, I don't want to bug you. Just wanted to tell you about another Stephenie Meyer book I started reading this week. It's called *The Host*. Who knew she had more books out?**

**Al: I just wanted to apologize one last time. Please don't avoid the club because of me. I have a terrible habit of sticking my foot in my mouth.**

For some reason, I was smiling as I read that last message. I wrote back:

**Me: You JUST NOW read The Host?! What sort of rock have YOU been living under? I absolutely loved that book. Look, I'm not mad. Just sensitive, I guess. I didn't mean to ghost you…I was just embarrassed. Can we be friends? I could really use one.**

So, that's how our daily conversations began. We talked about books, that's all. Until Martin started to question me about why I hadn't been knitting anything. *Why don't you try a little harder?* he said. So, I asked Al to help me with actual knitting. My first scarf turned out terrible, but Al didn't think so. I appreciated the encouragement, and after a while, knitting was sort of fun. We talked about knitting and we talked about books.

I didn't mention my marriage until after my arrest.

**Al: I'm so glad to see that you're online. It's been a while. You okay?**

**Me: Not really.**

**Al: Want to talk about it?**

**Me. Not really.**

**Al: I understand. For me, it's always been easier to forget. Even if you don't want to talk, I'm here any time you need me. You know that, right?**

**Me: I do. Thank you.**

I rubbed my cheeks until they burned, then I typed out another message. I clicked send before I changed my mind.

**Me: I went to jail.**

**Al: What?!!! What happened? Are you OK?**

**Me: I think I've been reading too many of these other members' stories. Lately, I've been standing up to him. It's like I recognize the abuse so easily now, and I can't tolerate it anymore. I just can't.**

**Al: What did he do?**

**Me: He locked me in our bedroom for two days. You know what's funny? I was afraid to bang on the door or scream. I was afraid one of the neighbors would call the cops and they'd take Lily away from me.**

**Al: Is Lily your daughter?**

**Me: Yes. Want to see a picture of her?**

**Al: I'd love to.**

I searched through my phone's photo album. I didn't have many of Lily, but the ones I did meant the world to me. I selected one of her eating spaghetti at the kitchen table. Her pink, plump cheeks had splotches of red sauce on them.

**Al: Aww she's gorgeous.**

**Me: Thank you.**

**Al: So, how did you get out of the bedroom?**

**Me: I begged him to let me out eventually. He couldn't handle**

watching Lily on his own for two days and he had to call into work. On the first day, he was daddy dearest: "Isn't it so much better without your mother here?" he asked her. But she knew I was in there. I mean, she's only three, but she's smart. She kept crying for me at the door and it ripped my heart apart. I try to buffer her from these things whenever I can…but it's impossible for her not to see it! He started getting frustrated with her and shouting at her not to cry. I was so scared, and I decided that when he opened that door, I was going to kill him. I scratched and clawed. I even tried to choke him. But then he gained the upper hand. He locked Lily in the room instead! And do you know what he did next? HE called the cops on ME. He told me to spend some time in jail thinking about what it means to be a good wife. He said that since Lily doesn't exist on paper (I gave birth to her at home on my own because he was convinced my previous midwife and other doctors' medical interventions could cause miscarriages), that it would be easy to make her not exist in real life. He said: I will kill her. KILL HER, Al. I was so scared. The whole time I was in that jail cell, I was so scared of what he might be doing to Lily, but I feared what he'd do if I tried to tell the cops my story. After all, he was the one with the marks on him, not me. If I leave, he'll kill me. But if I stay, he'll kill me too. And at this point, I don't care about me. I just want to keep my daughter safe. I thought by staying here with him, I was keeping her safer than if I tried to leave, but now…god I don't know, I'm rambling now.

Al: Jesus. I'm so damn sorry. That sounds like something out of a horror novel. Will you let me help?

Me: How? How can you help me?

Al: I don't know. But let's brainstorm ideas. We can make an escape plan. Together.

Me: But you don't understand. He has cameras outside, and this security app that alerts him when there's motion in the front, side, or back of the building. I tried to leave once while he was at work. I packed up some of our stuff and everything. We got less than a mile away, when he called me. I tried to speed up, but he caught up with me two towns over.

Al: Let's both think on it for a couple days and come up with ideas. We'll figure a way around all that, okay? We will do it together. I promise.

We spent the next couple months hashing out a few plans to get away from Martin. There were times when I didn't think I could do it. There were even times, good days with Martin, where I felt a tiny glimmer of hope, hope that he might change.

*But he still hasn't changed.* And as Lily gets older, I can't help wondering what sort of life she could ever have with Martin, even if he was less violent.

*I'm leaving for good this time. And the only person I can tell is Al.*

*Because I trust Al with my life.*

# CHAPTER THIRTY-TWO

*Al*

I fell in love with her, but that was never part of the plan. Sort of like when you sit down to read one chapter of a book and then, the next thing you know, the sun is coming up and you've read the whole damn thing. But that's a pretty lame analogy. Because Nova Nesbitt was so much more than a silly past time for me. We shared everything. Our secrets and fears. Her scars became mine and mine became hers. Eight hours was never enough, and it was never the full eight—she had to take care of the little girl, and knit something so that her husband wouldn't question why she spent all day using her Knitting Tips app.

So, I taught her how to actually knit. She was terrible at it, but I never told her so. And by the end, she was starting to make things that were actually recognizable. Sometimes, we'd listen to a song at the same time, or read passages from a book then talk about them. We tried to make pineapple upside down cakes from scratch, and hers turned out better than mine. We laughed about that for days; she never let me live down that picture of my soupy cake.

She sent me a few pictures of herself, but I never sent mine.

She was younger and more attractive than me, and that scared me.

I loved her, in the way you love your very best friend, but also so much more. I lived for those moments, talking to her...and I think she lived for them, too.

That's why I took the little girl. There was no choice in the matter. Running away from her crazy husband wasn't enough. Eventually, he would have found her and killed her. He would have killed them both, of that I had no doubt.

So, I did what I had to do to protect her. To protect them both. I don't regret that decision.

The first time I saw her, hair whipping in the wind as she stepped out of her shiny blue car, she sucked the breath from my chest.

# CHAPTER THIRTY-THREE

*The Neighbor*

## CLARA

In the den, I flipped on my television and perched on the edge of the couch, waiting for the nightly news. A few moments later, my fingers prickled, and a shiver crawled up my spine as I saw his name scrolling across the bottom of the TV screen. Martin Nesbitt, my tenant's husband, had been arrested on suspicion of kidnapping.

About time they focused on the right people and the right place, I thought, relieved. Martin Nesbitt looked like a killer, one of those never-thought-he-was-a-killer-because-he's-so-handsome types that always made me suspicious. Officer Ellie James was on the screen, too, leading a cuffed Martin Nesbitt into the police station.

"Can you tell us if these two missing women are related in some way?" a perky reporter shoved her mike at Officer James.

*Two women?* My stomach lurched. I was out of Camels, but I'd managed to find a stale pack of Parliaments downstairs. I lit one, puffing so hard I forgot to breathe through my nose. Finally,

I stood up from the couch and stubbed it out, just as a flicker of movement outside my window caught my eye.

Something bubbled up inside me as I tiptoed over to the window and leaned closer into the glass. The windowpane was behind my TV, so I couldn't get as close as I liked.

My own face peered back at me, murky and frightened. Am I scared of my own reflection now? Sheesh.

But then a white ghostly palm smacked the glass and I jumped back, screaming in terror.

# CHAPTER THIRTY-FOUR

## The Cop

### ELLIE

Staring through the thick glass window, I could literally feel my blood pressure rise.

"He's lying," I said, glancing over at Chad. "Can't you see it?"

Chad shrugged. "He seems to have a solid alibi for the night Nova went missing."

"And Lily," I snapped. "Don't forget about Lily."

"And Lily," Chad added, apologetically.

Through the glass window, I watched Officer Cummings interview Martin Nesbitt. They'd been in there for hours now and the man's composure hadn't faltered once. On the night Nova disappeared he had been showing houses to a local couple. It seemed ludicrous, that people would be house-hunting at night. But the Krowski couple had backed up Martin's alibi, much to my dismay.

"They're covering for him," I said, through gritted teeth.

"Possibly."

Officer Cummings was asking questions about Rachel Coffey now. Once again, Martin played dumb.

"I need in there. This might be Cummings' jurisdiction, but she disappeared from my town."

Martin gave me a sideways look as I entered the room. The corner of his lips twitched, as though he were holding back a smile.

"Like I was saying…I have no idea who Rachel Coffey is. I'll admit the picture you showed me looked a little familiar, but that's probably because I've seen her around. I see a lot of people… everyone knows me in Granton. Maybe I saw her at the grocery store, once or twice? Maybe that's it, I don't know. If my wife made an appointment with her, it's because of the miscarriage. She wanted to try again for another child, but I didn't. Maybe she met with Rachel behind my back, while I was at work, in order to get advice on conceiving another baby. Why in the world would I kill some woman I don't know, or had only seen in passing? It makes no sense. And while we're at it: why would I kill my wife? She left me, and that's what I asked her to do. Why would I ask her to leave, then chase her down and hurt her? Frankly, this whole thing baffles me. Especially the part about the little girl."

From my back pocket, I extracted the photograph I'd removed from the frame at the Nesbitt residence. I set it down on the table and pushed it toward him, then took a seat next to Officer Cummings.

Martin stared at the photo for several seconds, then looked back up. His eyes slid back and forth between Cummings and me.

"I don't get it. What am I supposed to be looking at here?"

"Right there." I tapped a finger on the doll, then the toys scattered on the floor in the background.

Martin glanced back down at the photo. His face revealed very little, but there was a tic in his right cheek. I could recognize a fellow jaw-clencher when I saw one…

"What's the matter, Martin? Am I making you mad?" I slammed my hands down on the table in front of him. He jumped back slightly, and I felt a tiny glimmer of satisfaction. Like my father and Ezra Clark, he wasn't used to women standing up to him.

Martin smiled and crossed his arms over his chest, recovering quickly.

"Not angry at all, ma'am. Officer Cummings and I were getting along just fine before you got here. These toys…I told you already, I have a niece. These must be hers. Why else would they be there…?"

"I thought you said it had been a long time since you saw your niece. This picture looks pretty recent. And what happened to your wife's cheek?"

Martin looked down at the photo again. "I have no idea what you mean." Again, his right cheek twitched.

"Your wife wrote a message to us in her own blood. She was afraid of you…afraid for herself and her daughter."

I could feel Cummings staring me down, a silent warning to cool it. Now I was the one flexing my jaw.

"How convenient that she would write that. Don't you understand? My wife was mentally ill. She obviously isn't above telling lies; after all, she did lie to the police about us having a child together. It's insane!"

"You're lying. And everyone in this room knows it…"

"I'll talk to you, and you only," Martin said, shifting his eyes back on Officer Cummings.

"Why? Because you don't like women standing up to you?" I jumped up from my seat, ready to hop across the desk and force him to tell me where Nova and Lily were…

"Only you or I want a lawyer," Martin said, through clenched teeth. He wouldn't even look at me now.

"I'm going," I said to Officer Cummings. "Going to get busy finding out where Nova and Lily are."

Outside the interrogation room, Chad was waiting. He was staring down at his shoes.

I placed my right cheek to the see-through glass, letting the cool relief rush over my angry, aching face.

# CHAPTER THIRTY-FIVE

*The Cop*

**ELLIE**

Heavy pounding poked my brain like a handful of needles. I sat up in my hotel bed, beer bottles clanking around in the covers beside me.

"Ugh." My head was blistery and throbbing from my late-night drinking session and probably from grinding my teeth in my sleep. While Roland and Mike had gone out to dinner, I'd holed up in my hotel room with a six-pack of Corona. Six beers were too much for me.

I rolled out of bed, knocking bottles on the floor and stumbling toward my overnight bag. "I'm coming, dammit."

My visitor banged and banged. "Just a sec!" I shoved myself into a pair of too-tight leggings and a YMCA t-shirt I'd brought along when I'd left for Granton in a hurry. "Who is it?" I asked, sliding the deadbolt from the door.

Martin Nesbitt had spent last night in jail. That was reason to celebrate, but I couldn't feel good about this case until Lily and Nova were found. Dead or alive.

"Good morning," I grumbled at Chad, who was perky and smiling despite the early morning hour. He had a bag of what appeared to be bagels in the crook of his arm and he thrust a cup of coffee at me.

"Come in." I took the coffee and bag from him, then led the way over to the small, lop-sided table in the corner of the hotel room. "This is my desk for the time being," I joked.

Chad sat down across from me. He waited until I'd added three packets of sugar to my coffee before he started talking. Immediately, I noticed that his speech was pressured, his eyes bloodshot. He seemed…more excited than usual, like he hadn't slept all night.

"What is it?" I asked, sitting my coffee back down on the desk. "Tell me."

"I've been up all night," Chad said, confirming my earlier thought. He was gripping the sides of the table, his knuckles turning white. "You're never going to believe what I found."

"Well, enlighten me then," I gushed. Adrenaline thrummed through my bloodstream. Could he prove Martin was a killer? Did he find out where Lily and Nova might be? I silently hoped.

"First, I looked at Martin's cell phone. Clean as a whistle, unless you consider soliciting online prostitutes suspicious."

"Why am I not surprised by that?" I picked my coffee back up and took a long sip. It tasted pumpkin-y and I blanched.

"He never deleted his history or tried to hide anything. If his wife was as paranoid and possessive as he claims, then you'd think he'd try to cover his tracks a little better, right?"

"Where was he soliciting them from?" I asked.

"An online website. Girls post pics of themselves, along with prices and either phone numbers or email addresses."

"How sad," I said, forcing down another sip of the spicy coffee. "So, he's a douche bag who cheats on his wife with prostitutes. That still won't help us find Lily and Nova though, Chad."

"Well, I haven't told you about Nova's phone yet," Chad said, scooting his chair up closer to the table. His eyes were round and bright, like two shiny pennies.

He cleared his throat. "Nova didn't have access to the internet, apparently. There was no internet set up in their apartment building. Yes, we found a wireless router when we searched. But it wasn't hooked up. Martin was using the internet provided by his cell phone provider. He apparently had some sort of parental controls set up on Nova's phone."

"That's disgusting," I hissed, pushing the coffee away for good this time. "And proves he was controlling and abusive..."

"Now here's the really interesting thing."

My throbbing head was buzzing with excitement now. "What is it?"

"Besides the normal apps that come on your phone, like weather, calendar, calculator, etcetera, she had only one app that had been manually downloaded. This knitting application, like an online club where you have access to patterns and knitting videos and shit," Chad said, excitedly.

"Sounds like a lot of fun," I said, flatly.

"Nova spent a lot of time on it. And when I say a lot of time, I mean a hell of a lot of time. Like sometimes eight hours a day, or more."

"Wow. I didn't see any knitting stuff in the apartment, did you? I mean, maybe a blanket or her bed pillows, but if she was knitting that much, that obsessed with it, you'd expect to see all kinds of knitted items around the apartment," I mused. "But you did say she had those markings on her teeth, so that part matches up."

"But what if the site wasn't for knitting? What if it was for something else?" Chad said, bubbling over with anticipation.

My eyes widened. "Like what?"

"It took all night, and a lot of favors from my hacker buddy in Chicago, but I got in. I can't see all the messages she sent yet, but I do know that she spent all her time talking to another user

182

named Al. It's an online shelter, Ellie, for victims who can't or won't go to a real one. It's pretty cool, actually."

"You think she's with this Al person, hiding out somewhere?" I asked. I stood up and started pacing. I thought about the mysterious truck parked at Widow's Curve. Could it belong to Al?

"It's very possible," Chad said, nodding vigorously.

He pushed Nova's cell phone across the desk. The site looked like a normal knitting site, at first glance. But it was so much more...

"And this is the person she's been talking to, non-stop." I stared at Al's profile. There was nothing in the profile that could help track this person down: no photos, no name or address...

"The internet service provider is Banshee. I can see it here," I said, tapping the ISP at the bottom of the browser.

"But how can we figure out who this user is in real life? We could send a message, but then, it might scare them off," Chad pondered.

"Well, we could get a warrant, subpoena Banshee...they have to tell us the IP address. And if we have the IP address, we can trace the physical address...maybe this Al knows where Nova is..."

Chad groaned. "Yeah, but how long will it take to get a warrant?"

"Too long. At least a few days..." I mulled. "But maybe...why don't we just go down there? I'm sure there's a Banshee hub around here." I used my own phone to search Google.

"Less than an hour away. Let's go," I said, my pulse quickening.

\*\*\*

I laid my badge on the counter, getting an instant reaction from the guy behind the counter at the Granton Banshee hub. They were a new-ish internet service provider; I'd never used them before, but I was hoping I could avoid the process of getting a warrant...

The guy behind the counter was young, and a stoner-type, with bloodshot eyes and long, stringy hair.

"Did I do something wrong?" the young man asked, his eyes flitting around the room, nervously.

"Oh, definitely not, sir. We're investigating two missing persons cases. We've tracked down a possible suspect in the crime, but we need an IP address. Do you think you could help me? This is time sensitive."

The guy looked around the empty office, still nervous.

"Okay, let me see it."

I sighed. I passed him Nova's phone. While he typed something into his own computer, I gave Chad a gleeful thumbs-up through the window. He was sitting in my cruiser in the parking lot, rocking with excitement.

"It will take fifteen or twenty minutes. Do you just need the IP address, or do you want the actual address of the IP user?"

I couldn't believe my luck. Smiling, I said, "Both please." For the first time since taking this case, I felt a glimmer of hope and excitement.

# CHAPTER THIRTY-SIX

## *Al*

She trusted me, which is why we planned her escape together. With the ad in the paper for the cabin in Northfolk, we both agreed: it was the perfect place. Out in the middle of nowhere and already partially furnished, it was far away from her family and friends. Far away from her abuser. Martin expected her to run toward her father and sister, and he expected her to leave while he was at work. So, we had to do the opposite.

At night, while he was sleeping comfortably, was the perfect time to do it. All she had to do was plant the blood evidence, but that was sort of tricky. She said it hurt, *a lot,* but I told her it was necessary. We had to take extra measures to make sure they suspected him. Who knew if they would use luminol in the apartment...but hopefully, they would, and then they would find her bloody message on the bathroom wall and the blood spots she left behind...

One week before she left, she waited until Martin and Lily were sleeping. In the bathroom, she locked the door and plugged the drain, then she slit both of her wrists. I told her how to do it so that she would bleed a lot, but not lose her own life. *It's all in how you cut,* I'd told her.

185

There was a small part of me that thought she wouldn't do it, but I'd never tell her that. The next day, she messaged me a picture that made my stomach turn. She'd lost enough blood to write the message and she'd scooped up the excess blood in the tub and splattered it around the living room and streaked it toward the kitchen. Afterwards, she wrapped her arms in gauze, and using heavy bleach, she stayed up all night scrubbing the evidence away. Martin beat her bad for the cutting, but she told him she was depressed because she wanted another baby. That sick bastard liked that for some reason. So, life in the Nesbitt household went on as normal for the next seven days.

She took only what she could throw together, even leaving the car seat behind. She turned his phone on silent so that his app wouldn't wake him up to alert him, and then her and Lily slipped out into the night. Before they left, she tossed Lily's extra pair of orange sneakers into the back of Martin's truck.

Halfway to Northfolk, she stopped and bought a cell phone. One of those disposable kind, just so no one could trace her. She texted me the number and told me to wait twenty-four hours, as we'd planned. I was so relieved when I got that text and knew she was close to safety.

I waited to call like she told me to, but I didn't wait to act. Leaving Martin wasn't enough. Unless the police had a reason to suspect him and search his home, he eventually would have found her. With his money and resources, it was only a matter of time.

So, I didn't have a choice. I had to take the girl. She needed to be somewhere safe, away from all the drama.

I slipped inside the cabin while they were both sleeping. The little girl barely stirred as I lifted her from the bed. I carried her out of the house, and as I cut through the woods behind the property, she opened her eyes and moaned for her mother.

# CHAPTER THIRTY-SEVEN

*The Neighbor*

## CLARA

After last night, I was afraid to go outside. With the windows locked and the curtains drawn tight, I felt a slight sense of relief. If I can't see out, then they can't see in, I assured myself as I made myself dinner in the kitchen. I was too nervous to eat, but my mother used to say that sometimes going through the motions can make you feel a little better when nothing else can.

Darkness had fallen over the farm like a warning shadow, and with the windows plastered shut, the house had assumed a foggy gloom akin to a cave. All of the stale cigarette smoke floating around didn't help much either. My throat felt blistery and sore.

Holding the butter knife, I slowly smeared Miracle Whip on six slices of bread. Suddenly, the knife clattered from my hand and hit the floor. A pair of headlights, deep red, pierced through the pearly white kitchen curtains even though they were closed.

I held my breath, waiting. Listening. Finally, I heard the soft thud of a door slamming and then a gentle knock at the door. Nervously, I crept over to the peephole. Taking a deep breath, I looked out to see who it was.

It was only Officer James. As usual, she looked like a nervous Nancy. I considered not answering, pretending to be asleep, but I wanted to hear an update about Martin Nesbitt and what happened to him in Granton.

Finally, I placed my hand on the knob and pulled the front door open while wearing a wooden smile. "Saw you on the news last night. You made it back to town pretty quickly."

"We need to talk, Clara."

Officer James' usual nervousness was all but gone, her face now grim and daunting.

"Okay. Come in." I headed for the kitchen to sit down, but she was already talking as I turned my back.

"Where did you take the girl? And what did ya do to Nova Nesbitt?"

My mouth dropped open and I turned around. "What the hell are you talking about?"

"We know about the website. The secret knitting club. We know you were the one chatting with her in Tennessee. I know you lured her here as your renter. Shit, you probably showed her your own ad in the paper. But why? If you cared about her so much, why would you take her little girl?"

I shook my head in disgust. "You're insane. I've never even met Nova. She mailed in her deposit, and we spoke by email twice when she was interested in renting the property. She disappeared before I even got to meet her, you know?"

"No, I don't know that. You knew her well, didn't you, Clara? All those conversations between her and *Al*. Between her and *you*."

"Al? I don't know anyone named Al!" I snapped, pressing my back against the kitchen counter. The edge of it felt sharp as a razor against my back, and I pressed harder, wishing this woman would leave.

"Your little sister who got sick and died when you were a kid. Her name was Allison, right? You called her Al. My mother told me that. And you had a daughter who died, tragically, too. Were you trying to replace your daughter with Nova's?"

"Of course not!" The room tilted and swayed sideways, like I was upside-down at the fair. I closed my eyes, wishing the spinning would go away.

"And that's not the only thing we found. I got the VIN number off the truck. I know it belongs to your sister. Did she help you hide the girl? Did she help you hide the body? Is your sister here right now?"

Officer James was serious, her hands on her hips, lips curled up in a nasty smile. Any trace of that anxious woman I met the other day was gone.

"I told you. I don't know what you're talking about." I stumbled around the kitchen until I found my cigarette pack. But my hands were shaking so bad, I couldn't light one.

"Oh, but you do, Clara. Your sister, Rachel, and your daughter, Krissy, are involved with a website that helps victims of domestic violence. I know you guys think you were doing the right thing by taking Nova's child, but you weren't. You can't just take someone's baby. I wish you'd just talk to me. Explain what's going on…"

My throat tightened in dread. "Rachel? What does Rachel have to do with any of this? It's my daughter Krissy's website; Rachel just helps refer women who are in trouble to the site…"

Officer James cursed under her breath. "He really must have done it."

"Done what?" I asked, my voice as small as a child's. "Has something happened to Rachel?"

"I'm sorry to tell you this but Rachel is also missing," she said. "So, cut the crap. I know you knew Nova before she became your *tenant*."

"Then he killed her. That awful man must have killed her," I moaned. My feet wobbled out from under me and I dropped down to my knees. Had Nova's awful husband murdered my sister? I wouldn't put it past him…

I flopped forward onto the kitchen floor, burying my face into the sandy linoleum as the pain washed over me.

# CHAPTER THIRTY-EIGHT

**72 hours earlier**

*The Mother*

## NOVA

"Al? I-is that r-really you?" I stammered into the phone. I was out of bed now, pacing, eager to talk to her on the phone for the very first time.

Her voice was gravellier than I'd expected, and she sounded scared. The fact that Al was scared, scared the hell out of me. But then she started talking, started explaining herself, and everything fell in line.

*She'd taken my daughter.*

"God, Al, I fr-freaked the f-fuck out. I c-called the cops and everything. I th-thought Martin took her."

"He didn't, but I needed you to call the cops. We need them to have an excuse to search his apartment, you know? They'll find the blood and the shoes in the backseat. That should be enough right there to make a jury distrust him. And, now he knows where you are, so you must get going. That police woman

191

called him and so did you. It won't take long for him to track you down, he could already be on the way," Al said. The fear in her voice was gone, replaced with stone-like seriousness. "You still there, Nova?"

*It still feels strange hearing her say my real name.*

"I g-got to g-get the hell out of here. He's c-coming, you're r-right. Is she okay? P-please say my baby's okay. I d-don't want her to be too scared."

"She's fine, I promise. Rachel left the truck in the spot. You remember the plan we discussed, right?" she asked.

I took a deep breath and closed my eyes, remembering. "In the w-woods, near the tree th-that looks evil and twisted, I have to d-dig up the c-containers. Sp-splatter them around, dr-drop the t-teeth I saved on the floor, and th-then p-put the containers and my cell phone into the d-duffel bag."

"You put the rocks in there, right? The heavy ones from your garden? It needs to be heavy, you know? We need that bag to sink, so that no one finds the cell phone or the containers…" Al explained.

"It's lined with the r-rocks," I assured her. "Now where's the v-vehicle again?"

"Parked less than half a mile down the road. Keys should be in it. And there's a map to where you're going and a new cell phone in the glove box. Just drive, okay? Don't stop to dump the bag until you're at least two states away."

"Okay. Th-thank you, Al. How long will it be t-till you c-come t-too?" I asked, my voice shaky with emotion. *I love her.* When I imagined falling in love, I never expected it to be this intense, this unbelievably painful and good, all at the same time. And so different than how it was with Martin…

"I don't know. I'll need to stay a while, so it doesn't look too suspicious. We don't want them to connect us somehow. But we'll talk as soon as you get to Krissy's house okay? I know you don't know her well, but she's my daughter so you have to trust her.

You can stay with her and her husband as long as you need. You need to get going now. I love you."

"I l-love you, too," I choked. I held the phone away from my head and forced myself to press 'end'.

Immediately, I sprang into action, pulling on my jeans and a pair of boots. In the laundry room, there were gardening supplies. I grabbed a small shovel and brought it with me.

As I pulled the duffel bag across the back lawn, chills ran up my spine. I stopped pulling and looked all around me, spinning in circles, unable to shake the feeling that I was being watched.

Through the woods, I kept my ears perked as I located the twisted tree Al told me about. Supposedly, she had scoped out the property and cabin when she found the ad in the paper. She'd come out here at dark and buried the containers of cow blood for me.

The fact that I was standing somewhere Al had been made me want to lie down on the ground and cry. But I kept going, thrusting my shovel into the hard, cold soil at the base of the tree. The cannisters were full of dark, rosy liquid and in the moonlight, they sparkled and shone, as I loaded them into the rock-filled duffel bag. It was so heavy on the way back, that I was panting and sweating.

Back inside, I closed the door behind me. I still couldn't shake the feeling that Martin was close and coming soon. It wouldn't take him as long to reach West Virginia as it did me…I imagined him in his truck, foot to the floor and eyes ablaze as he charged across the country to find me.

In the living room, I unlatched the bloody cannisters. The blood came out faster than I thought it would, forming a strangely circular blot in the center of the room. It reminded me of one of those inkblot tests they used to use back in the day.

*What do you see, Nova? What does this look like, and what does that say about you?*

I knelt on the floor next to the massive blood puddle and I

tried to wipe the blood around and spread it out wider. Next, I retrieved the broken teeth from a Ziploc bag in my kitchen drawer. Because of Martin, I'd lost three teeth. When he smacked me or squeezed my face, they just got looser each time. Originally, I'd saved them hoping I could get them fixed. But now, I was putting them to a better use…

I grabbed the duffel bag from the floor and took one last look at the cabin. "Thanks for your help," I told it, for once not struggling to say the words. Then I slipped out the front door, leaving it unlocked behind me.

# CHAPTER THIRTY-NINE

*The Cop*

## ELLIE

"You have to believe me," Clara moaned from the floor. It looked like the news that her sister was missing had caused real, physical pain. She was writhing on the floor as though she were in agony.

"Tell me what happened. I need to know."

"Martin always said he'd make Lily disappear if Nova tried to leave him. She wanted to run away with Lily, go stay with my daughter… It was only supposed to be temporary. We had a plan and Rachel wanted to help us. Rachel and I are sisters, but we haven't been close in years…but then…well, we both cared about Nova. Rachel was her midwife during her first pregnancy. For a long time, Rachel suspected she and Lily were being abused…

"Rachel agreed to drive down here and leave Nova the truck. She bought it cheaply from one of her former clients, another member of the site…"

I put up a hand to stop her. "Why didn't Nova just drive her own car? This is weird."

But Clara was shaking her head. "The Celica was in Martin's

name, just like everything else they owned. We couldn't put it past him that he might report it stolen, or even have a tracking device on there…"

"Okay. Keep going," I urged her.

"The truck was an escape vehicle for Nova. Rachel was supposed to come back to my house afterwards, to arrange a rental car back home. But she never showed up, and then I heard about the truck just sitting there…I guessed Martin had got them. All three of them…" Clara started wailing again.

"So, Rachel delivered Nova's baby? Lily was real, then."

Clara let out a strange laugh. "Of course, she's real. Like I said, Rachel was Nova's midwife during her first pregnancy. But then she lost the baby. A baby boy named Matthew. Martin blamed her for losing the baby. He wanted a child so badly…and he also didn't want Nova getting any medical help with Lily's birth. Rachel did an ultrasound for her, but then she just assumed Nova got a different doctor…that wasn't the case though. Martin forced her to deliver the baby all on her own. Lily was born on the bathroom floor. Even Martin didn't stay by her side. He didn't want anyone involved. He was practically holding them prisoner! But then, Nova needed a babysitter, so she called Rachel. Technically, Rachel was the only person who could verify Lily's existence—besides Nova and Martin, she's the only other living soul who's laid eyes on her. Do you think that's why Martin took my sister?" Clara's face crumbled.

"How did you connect with Nova on the website? Did Rachel ask you to do that, to reach out to her?"

Clara shook her head. "No, I've always been a member of Krissy's website. In fact, I was one of the first members. My husband was abusive, so you see…Krissy was inspired to help women like me because she grew up in an abusive household."

My cell phone buzzed in my pocket and I turned away to take the call.

"Sergeant, I'm so glad you called. I—what? Okay, I'm on my

way." I pointed at Clara and said, "Don't move a muscle till I get back. I'm serious."

"Where are you going?" Clara pleaded.

It almost hurt me to say it because I could tell she was hurting. "That was Sam. They think they just found Nova's body."

# CHAPTER FORTY

*80 hours earlier*

*Martin*

She was beautiful as she ran. Long, dark legs and shorts so short, they ended where her ass stopped, and her legs began. Killing her served only one purpose—she was a loose end. But even if she wasn't, running around like that at night, she was simply asking for it.

I hired Rachel Coffey as a midwife for my first child because she came highly recommended and because she was attractive. I hoped she might have an affair with me, but as it turned out, she was a prude. She was also careless. She couldn't keep my son alive. There was no way I'd let her be involved in my daughter's birth. Plus, I'd read somewhere that if you birthed a child without medical assistance, then you legally didn't have to file a birth certificate. If Lily didn't exist on paper, then she didn't have to exist in real life...if Nova tried to run and take my daughter, I could kill her and keep my daughter, without anyone knowing she was alive. Or I could make them both disappear if I had to.

Now that time had arrived: Nova had run away, taking my

daughter with her. It was only a matter of time before I tracked them both down. Punishing Nova would be fun when I found her...

But first I had to take care of Rachel. She was the only one that could prove my daughter's existence. And I had a sneaking suspicion that Rachel was the one who helped her get away. Who else? Nova didn't have any friends, and I'd made sure to keep her separated from her family.

Before I could get my girls back, I had to tie up this loose end...

I'd watched Rachel before, many times, fantasizing about how it would feel to tear her pretty little body apart. And it's a good thing I did, because now I knew that she took evening runs at least three nights per week, usually at the same time.

And I knew beyond a shadow of a doubt that she was involved in helping Nova escape.

Jim and Jane Krowski needed a new house and I needed an alibi. The refurbished colonial on Vermouth was a good choice—I chose it specifically because the woods behind it connected with Deer Place Park, and Deer Place Park connected with the bike path.

So, while the Krowskis, with their too-tan, cracked skin and tummy-tucked waists, banged one out in the master bedroom I was trying to sell, I slipped out the back door. If they fucked as long as they did last time, then I had more than enough time to get the job done, and then I could go get Nova...

I watched through the trees as Rachel approached the bike path. As she curled around the corner, legs gliding like a prized filly at the Kentucky Derby, I stepped out from the shadows onto the path behind her. Immediately, she either heard or sensed me there. When she turned around, ponytail swishing back and forth, she froze when she saw it was me. The look on her face was priceless. I could almost taste her fear.

Her eyes flitted down to the knife in my hand. Her mouth

opened into an O of horror, then she turned around and took off running. This should be a challenge, I thought, sarcastically.

It took me only a few seconds to catch her. She kicked, and she fought, slamming the backs of her heels against my shins. I squeezed my hands around her neck, long enough to make her go unconscious but not enough to kill her.

After dragging her body off the path, I carried her through the woods to the closest shelter bathhouse and locked us both in a stall. For fifteen minutes, she held out. The knife always does the trick...

She told me about her plans to take the truck to Northfolk, West Virginia. She even gave me the keys to the truck and revealed their little crummy "plan".

I stabbed her once because I'd always wanted to try it, but she was still alive when the flames rose.

Through the hot glowing body of fire, I watched her. Admired the way her body twisted and curled, like an exotic dance she performed only for me. I kept watching, never blinking, until the life was sucked from her chest.

The feeling it gave me could only be described as exhilaration.

By the time I made it back to the Krowskis, covered in sweat and panting, the keys to Rachel's truck curled in my hand, they could only assume that I'd been enjoying their little performance as much as they had hoped.

But all I could think about as I shook their hands and smiled, was how sexy Rachel looked, even in death. If it felt this good killing a woman I barely knew, I couldn't imagine how good it would feel when I finally killed my wife.

# CHAPTER FORTY-ONE

**71 hours earlier**

*The Mother*

## NOVA

I reached the truck in under a quarter mile, but it felt like walking across the Sahara with that big bag in tow. Fear surged through my veins. I was afraid Martin would pull up beside me and force me into his truck, or worse yet, mow me down. But I had to stay strong.

Most people think that abused women are weak, and I used to think that, too. Until I became one. The women I met on that website were strong. *And right now, I've never felt stronger*. It took a lot of strength and endurance to make it through my marriage alive. Every day...the tolerance, restraint, and fear I endured, made me feel more sturdy than weak.

I'd dreamed about this moment for a long time, and now it was finally happening. I could almost see Lily running around outside, baking under the sun...*Oh, how I cannot wait to get there with her.*

The truck bloomed before me as I curled around a windy curve, and I was pleased to find it unlocked when I walked up on it. *Thank you for doing this, Rachel. Without you and Al, I never could have pulled this off...*

*I just have to keep the faith and follow the plan. I can do this. I can do my part...*

I tossed my bag inside and scooted it over in the passenger seat. I leaned in and opened the glove box. As promised, there was a map inside with an address for where I was going and a new disposable cell phone.

*Cell phone!* "Oh, god! Dammit! Dammit!" I slapped the steering wheel and jumped back out, pulling the bag out too. I'd left the cell phone on the bedroom dresser after I'd hung up with Al. If I left it behind, they could trace the call and find her. They might even find Lily!

*I was supposed to put the phone in the bag, Al had told me that a hundred times!*

The police could find it. Or worse, Martin might find Al.

I considered leaving the heavy bag behind, but what if that police officer came and found the truck sitting here while I was running back to get the phone? I made a quick decision, to take the bag. Closing and locking the truck, I started the hellish trek back to the cabin.

My arms were numb and burning from the heavy load, but I pushed harder this time.

*I have to hurry up and get back to the truck.*

The road swayed, the cabin in the distance growing smaller and smaller. Silently, I counted, trying to focus on my daughter and Al. *I can't lose it and freak out now! I'm almost home-free.*

Several minutes later, I was standing in front of the cabin again. *Martin could be on his way to Northfolk by now. I have to get going...*

It was a grisly thought, but I had no choice. I needed to get that phone. I had to dump the entire bag. *I only hope the stones are heavy enough to weigh it down...we can't leave any evidence behind that we staged this...*

Gripping the car keys in my hand, I dragged the bag around to the back of the cabin. I left it leaning against the back door, securing it tight in case Martin showed up and tried to sneak in on me. Through the dark cabin, I ran through the kitchen and down the hallway. The phone set on the dresser, taunting me. *I can't believe I almost forgot it!*

I grabbed the phone and ran back to the back door. I was about to drop it in the bag when suddenly, I saw a stream of headlights poking through the trees. Someone was coming up the road from the other side. *They will reach the cabin in a matter of minutes!*

My body jolted with fear. The headlights looked just like the ones on Martin's truck, or so I imagined. I gripped the keys and cell phone, leaving the bag behind, then shot out the front door, running for my life back toward the windy curve where the truck set.

By the time I came around the bend, the headlights were right behind me.

*I only need to go a few more feet. I could outrun him in the truck if I had to*, I thought, my thoughts whirling out of control.

But then blue and red lights flickered on top of the vehicle.

*A police car. Officer James had picked a bad time to check on me now!*

But this was good news. It wasn't Martin, and as long as I could get her to turn back around, I'd have enough time to go back for the bag I'd just left behind. The cell phone was still gripped tightly in my hand. Did I really need to go back for those cannisters? Al's instructions repeated in my mind. *Dammit.*

The police lights flickered again and this time, I started walking toward them. The lights were blinding, and they pulsated, their rhythm pulsating inside of me...

I didn't want Officer James to turn the corner and find the

strange truck parked back there. *What will I do if she sees it? Should I tell her it's mine?* My thoughts were spinning out of control.

The police cruiser slowed to a stop as I approached the driver's window. The window rolled down and a police officer I'd never seen before looked out at me.

"Get in," he ordered.

# CHAPTER FORTY-TWO

## *The Cop*

### ELLIE

She was here in Northfolk all along. Strangely, as I peered over the shoulder of the medical examiner and other officers at the scene, I couldn't help thinking her face looked serene, almost peaceful.

Lips curled up, almost as though she were smiling, and hair spread out around her face like a shiny black halo of feathers. It was her body that told a different story. It was blackened and burned, her arms and legs curled up to her torso like a newborn baby.

Sergeant DelGrande said, "They've collected evidence here, and around the woods, but there's still more to do. If there were footprints, the rain must have washed them away, though…"

"That isn't Nova Nesbitt." I choked the words out, holding my hand up to my face to combat the overpowering smell of charred flesh.

"What did you say?" Sergeant DelGrande knelt down beside me.

"I recognize her face from the photo. This is Rachel Coffey, the other missing woman from Granton."

Sarge stood up and walked off to make a phone call. When he returned minutes later, I was still mesmerized by the doll-like mask that was Rachel's face.

*Clara was right—her sister is dead. But where are Nova and Lily?*

As though he were reading my mind, Sergeant DelGrande said, "These guys have been combing through every square inch of these woods. We haven't found any other bodies. Why don't you go home and get dressed? It's cold out here. You haven't even been home since getting back from Granton, right? You don't need to see her like this," he told me, delicately.

"I'm fine. I don't see you telling Mike or Roland or anyone else to go 'get dressed'," I snapped, angrily.

"Okay then. Well, the medical examiner is going to take her now. If you want to meet us down there in a few hours for the autopsy, you can." He gave me a tight smile.

"I'll see you then," I said, bitterly.

I headed back to my cruiser, mind reeling. If the medical examiner could determine that she'd died on Saturday night, then Rachel Coffey died around the same time Nova went missing.

*Could Nova be involved in her former midwife's death? Or possibly Clara?*

It seemed unlikely, but still…

My mind drifted back to the farm and Clara Appleton. I hadn't even told the Sergeant yet about her connection with Nova. I was about to turn back and go tell him, when I had a thought: Martin probably killed all three of them. *Nova, because she left him. Rachel, because she knew about Lily. But Lily…no. Why would he go to the trouble of covering up her existence if he was simply going to kill her?*

My thoughts turned around and around, going nowhere.

Inside my cruiser, I laid my head against the steering wheel.

"I'm sorry, Nova. I'm so sorry I wasn't there to answer your call. If I had, maybe I could have helped you. We've found Rachel, but where are you…?" I pulled my phone from my pocket, staring down at the buttons until they looked wavy and foreign.

*Why couldn't I have been the one to take her call that night? Why?!*

I'd never listened to the voicemails she'd left on the on-call cell phone the night she vanished. Over the past couple days, I'd been so swept up in looking for evidence at the Nesbitt residence, that I hadn't bothered to listen or look close to home. Somehow, listening now seemed like a bad idea…listening to a possibly dead woman's distress calls…

But listening was the least I could do.

I clicked on the voice messages and held the phone to my ear. A robotic woman's voice informed me that I had zero messages. "Roland, you prick." I clenched my jaw, my face reddening with anger.

Roland was probably worried he'd get in trouble for not responding to an emergency call and had deleted the messages. Disappointed, I flipped through the call log, trying to figure out what time she'd called. I scrolled through, stopping when I saw her number on the screen. Nova had called at 11:03 on Saturday night. I expected to find it listed as a missed call, since Roland said he got the messages on Sunday morning. But instead, I was shocked to see that the call had lasted for twenty-six minutes.

I tried to imagine Roland down at the bar and the strip club, accidentally bumping the phone while he was stumbling around drunk. Or what if…?

I pulled out my personal cell and dialed Mike. "Pick up, pick up…" I chanted.

"Hello?" He was somewhere out there with the rest of the guys, combing for evidence in the trees.

"Mike, it's Ellie. You and Roland were out drinking on Saturday, right?"

"Yeah, why?" He sounded far away, his voice tinny and strange.

"Were you together all night? I'm trying to coordinate Rachel Coffey's death with the time Nova called the on-call line."

"Oh, okay. Yeah, he got a call that he responded to. I told him he was too drunk to go, but you know how well he listens. He's not in trouble, is he?" Mike sounded grave serious now, always looking out for his buddy.

"No. Just trying to figure out some details for this case. You said he left? About what time?"

"About 11:30, why? These questions are weird, Ellie. You're making me uncomfortable." I could almost see him shaking his head on the other line.

"Did you see him again after that? Did he come back to the bar?"

"No. He went home after checking on a domestic call. Said he was wiped out. Ellie, why don't you call Roland and just ask him? I d— "

I hung up too fast to hear his last words.

# CHAPTER FORTY-THREE

*The Cop*

**ELLIE**

Driving in West Virginia had always come naturally to me. When I first got my license, the hills were so steep at times that it felt like I'd never reach the top, and other times, they'd decline so sharply that I couldn't slow down, and there was this constant fear of flying down, down, down, right off the edge of the mountains when I reached the bottom. But over time, I'd grown accustomed to them, even learning to love the rise and fall of the rocky terrain. A million times I'd made these turns, a dozen different versions of me, and now I barely used my brake around the curly mountain edges or flinched when I rolled wildly downhill.

But tonight, everything had changed. Everything looked different. I noticed the rickety signs, the dangerous curves, and the mark of poverty and decay. Featureless shadows danced through the trees as I followed the windy, mountain roads that cut between them. The blurring vegetation became so disorienting at times, like I was driving through a tunnel made of trees and there was no end in sight. I imagined him out there somewhere, Martin Nesbitt or maybe someone else, sliding between the shadows, lurking in my own backyard…

It was easier to stomach tragedy when it happened somewhere else. But this felt too close…like if it could happen in Northfolk, it could happen to me, or someone I cared about.

I didn't know Rachel Coffey. But she could be any of us…like Nova, like Mandy Clark…the victim of a monster. In my mind, the monster I was looking for was Martin Nesbitt. But then his face evaporated, and he became all the other men in my life: Roland, even my own father…

As I passed Widow's Curve, old stories came rushing back to me…

Supposedly, the sharp curve was haunted, or cursed in some way. I'd never believed the stories before, but now that a woman was dead, I couldn't help but wonder. I'd heard several different versions of the story that made the legend behind the name, but my mother told me the true story once…

A woman and a man were engaged to be married, but she didn't love him. He said he loved her, but what he really meant was that he wanted her to be his. *You're mine forever,* he'd told her, on the night they were engaged. His family had money and power, and the girl's parents and sister tried to force her to marry the guy. *If you won't, I will,* the sister threatened. But on the day of the wedding, they couldn't get the soon-to-be bride to go. She said, *I don't think I can do it, not for all the money or comfort in the world.* Somehow the guy caught wind of it, that she wasn't coming, so he charged crazily through the streets of Northfolk, knocking over mailboxes and signs, looking for the girl that he had already claimed to be his. The girl's family finally talked her into going. *This is your fate,* they said. *Don't you believe in destiny?* So, she got in her car and drove to the church, but before she could get there, she was met by her future-husband in the road. At the curl of the curve, she parked her car and he parked his.

210

When she got out, she could see how angry he was. She tried to say she was sorry, that she'd changed her mind and he could have her, but he shoved her. He shoved her so hard...she fell right near the edge of the mountain. But as she stumbled back, teetering on her heels by the edge, she grabbed the tie on his shirt. Together, they toppled over, crashing to their death below. The family, so distraught and worried about what others would think of them, pushed their cars off the edge and called it a tragic accident.

I blinked, remembering the story my mother told me, as I stared at the eerie scenery around me. *So many different versions of the same stories...how can anyone know the truth anymore?*

As the trees grew sparser, I realized I'd been holding my breath this whole drive.

*Nothing feels safe anymore. Not in this town; not anywhere. Will it ever feel safe again?* I lamented.

I pulled up outside the Appleton Farm, willing myself to get out of my car and go inside. The last thing I wanted to do was tell a woman that her sister was dead...not just dead but murdered brutally. And her online partner was most likely dead as well...

I tried to shake away the flashing images of Rachel's masked face, the burns on her torso and hands...

The curtains of the farmhouse were drawn, but there were lights coming from the kitchen. This time, when I knocked, I did it softly, part of me hoping she had gone to sleep, so I could avoid this part of my job.

I could hear Clara on the other side of the door, fiddling with the locks.

When she opened the door, she looked more put together than she had when I'd left her. Clara's gray-streaked hair was twisted back in a tight knot at the base of her skull and her face looked shiny, although still red and splotchy from crying.

"She's dead, isn't she? I already know my sister's gone, I can feel it bone-deep."

I nodded. "I'm sorry for your loss, but we need to talk some more, Clara. There's still two people missing."

I expected her to drop to the floor, sobbing, again. But her face looked hard, resolute. She dropped her arms to her sides and turned around, leading me through the kitchen and into the dim-lit den. The den was full of black, industrial-sized garbage bags. Toys spilled out from the top of one bag, overflowing onto the floor.

"I'm clearing out stuff I don't need anymore. My kids are gone, dead or all grown up...no need for all of this..." Clara said, wringing her hands together. She looked spacey, lost...

I stared at a tattered old doll on the floor. There was a tiny pink brush beside it, like the kind I used to use to make all my barbies perfect and presentable.

There were things grinding in my head, spinning ceaselessly. Gnawing to come out. Something about that doll made me feel uneasy. The glossy body with the bent-back posture and too-small waist, its eyes so depthless and its mouth flat. Like a pretty, perfect, lifeless girl that's only purpose in life was to be played with. *You could bend them and brush them, make them do what you want...*

Had Roland tried to make Nova Nesbitt do what he wanted? He was probably drunk and horny when that call had come in. He'd told me he hadn't answered it, that he'd missed the call...but that wasn't true. The log showed that he was on the phone with Nova for twenty-six minutes. *Twenty-six minutes!* Maybe nothing happened, but why did he lie about that call...?

I closed my eyes, remembering that day when I got there. In her robe, so soft and pink, and her mental state so fragile. Not bendable but broken.

Suddenly, I was hurtling back to the academy in Illinois. So excited to have been picked, so excited to prove myself...and when the lead instructor asked me to come alone with him to his office, I actually beamed with pride. Because I'd had a good day that day, hitting more than half my shots and I could outrun

212

most of the guys on the obstacle course. I didn't need extra help or special treatment, I was just as good as the rest of them. He told me he was proud of me. He told me I was a star. He said all the things I wanted, and needed, to hear. And at first, I didn't notice the weird breathiness in the way he talked, or the bulge pluming from his pants. But I noticed when he slid his hand up the front of my shirt and under my bra. I was frozen in time, frozen in place, as he pinched my nipple hard. *Just let me touch them, okay? Let me feel them, baby. Oh yeah. You like that, don't you?* I pulled my shirt down and left his office, but that was all I did. The next day, I showed up for training. I never told a soul. And I didn't think about it because for some reason I felt like if I didn't think about it, then maybe it didn't really happen.

Maybe I never said anything about my instructor because I was ashamed. Or…maybe, it was *worse* than that. Maybe I kept it to myself because it was so commonplace, so expected, so *un*shocking, that I didn't feel the need to share. That realization frightened me more than anything…that I'd become so comfortable, so *dulled*, to a society that used, abused, and mistreated its women.

I used to wish for breasts and curves and first kisses…but then I just wanted it all to go away for a while. Even now, it's still this slippery balance beam that I haven't learned to walk on yet…

But Roland isn't my instructor, I reminded myself. There's no proof that he did anything to Nova. Was I just being paranoid? He was an asshole. He, and the other guys, didn't trust me because I'd shot and killed one of their own. But that didn't make him a killer or a kidnapper…and Clara Appleton was hiding something, more than she was telling…

Shuddering, I looked down and realized I was covering my chest with my hands.

"Do you want to go on the back porch and talk? I need some air," Clara said.

213

There was nothing I wanted more than to escape this sad, stuffy farmhouse but I had to figure out what Clara knew. Did she know where Nova and Lily were?

"Okay," I said.

I followed Clara out the back door off the den and stepped out onto a narrow wooden porch that overlooked the back of the property. Long, rolling fields with a back drop of woods. A slanted barn stood in the distance, leaning so far left I was surprised to find it still standing.

"Did you see any cop cars that night? The night Nova went missing? I know you said you saw a truck, but that was before I knew you were involved," I said, dully.

"I didn't see any truck, or any cop cars for that matter. Besides your visit on the morning Lily went missing, and again, on Sunday morning when you found the blood inside the cabin."

"What about the truck you said you saw? Was any of it true?" I asked.

Clara eyes were fixated on the barn, as though she could see something there that I couldn't.

"The truck belongs to Rachel. The plan was for Nova to leave the evidence behind to frame Martin, and then her and Lily were going to get the hell out of dodge."

"Well, I don't think they made it, Clara. And we certainly know Rachel didn't," I said, emotionless as I looked over at the cabin. It was dark and gloomy, the saddest house I'd ever seen, and it was hard to believe that there had been so many cop cars parked out there the other day. Hard to believe that only a few days ago, Nova and her daughter were moving in. They probably felt safe, at least for a little while…

"Where did they find my sister? Can you tell me how she died?" Clara asked. The wind rushed through the trees of the forest, swaying dangerously from side to side.

"They found her out past Widow's Curve, about thirty feet east, in that patch of trees behind the old sawmill road. She was under a peach tree. If it's any consolation, she looked peaceful," I said, softly. Images of her rippling, shadowy cheeks and the curled-up hands fluttered through my head. I tried to blink them away.

"And cause of death?"

"We won't know that until an autopsy's done. I'm headed there when I leave here. But, it wasn't a natural death, that much is certain."

For the first time since we'd walked outside, Clara turned her body and faced toward me. "Am I going to jail?"

I considered her question but didn't answer. "The bunny. Who put it there in the cabin? My sergeant said it was you. He said your husband used to make those things. Where is he?"

With shaky hands, Clara took out a pack of cigarettes. She offered me one, but I declined. Taking a deep drag, she said, "I put it there before they moved in. It was for the girl. I knew about her daughter and I just wanted to give her something," Clara explained, squeezing her eyes closed at the last part.

"So, was Lily Nesbitt really missing? Or was that all part of the plan?"

Clara frowned. "It wasn't the plan at first but now they're all gone...will you lock him away for good? Can you promise me that?"

I couldn't give her an answer.

"What about the shoes in Martin's back floorboard? How did those get there?"

Clara's eyes popped open. "Part of the plan. Martin ordered most of Lily's clothes and shoes online. He never even let Nova get on the internet, you know that?"

I nodded.

"Well, Nova started asking him to buy doubles of things. Shoes that fit Lily really well, or shirts that she'd grown fond of. So, on the day she left, she tossed the shoes in the backseat."

"What about the clothes and toys and books? Why all the new stuff for Lily if she was going to leave town so soon?"

Clara puffed on her cigarette, nodding. "I bought that stuff before they moved in. I knew they wouldn't have time to pack up much, and I wanted to make sure Lily had some things. That little girl has been through a lot, you know? I went a little overboard, I'll admit. I knew Nova couldn't take it all with her when they left town, but I figured I'd pack it away when I got the cabin back and send it to them when they got to Texas."

"And the blood? She put that there herself, so we'd find it? This all just sounds so…crazy," I sighed.

"What's crazy is the fact that so many women in this country have to go to extraordinary lengths to escape from abusive men. Did you know that if a woman divorces her abuser and files for a restraining order, her chance of being killed *increases*? The only way to get help is to escape and pray that the abuser either goes to jail or moves onto another victim. Nova was scared to death of that man. Do you think we would have done all this if there was any other way?"

Her words pierced like a knife. I was part of this failing system she referred to. I just couldn't accept her words as truth…surely, there was another option?

"I wish Rachel wouldn't have come. He must have followed her, or hell, he may have killed her before she ever left town…"

"I don't have those answers yet, Clara, but hopefully I will soon. In the meantime, I need to find Nova and her little girl…"

"Martin has a good job and he's well-liked in Granton. His face is plastered over half the city. What if there's not enough evidence to convict him? If he has an alibi and there's no DNA, no fibers…he'll walk for my sister's death. He'll walk for all of it…This shit happens every day and you guys do nothing. People get locked up for smoking pot. Meanwhile, men like Martin Nesbitt walk free. It's sickening."

I twisted my hands together, considering her words.

"Did you go over there and help her with the blood? Why weren't you there by her side during this getaway process?" I asked, still trying to wrap my head around the details.

Clara's face scrunched up, collapsing in on itself. "I was always honest with Nova, until I wasn't. There's only one lie that I told… when I sent her the ad in the paper, I didn't tell her that her landlord was me. She only ever knew me as Al."

"But why? Why would you be so deceptive?" She's still hiding something. Maybe she killed Nova. Hell, maybe she killed her own sister. Who is this woman, really? I wondered.

"If Nova had known I was right next door, I don't think she would have left town. I wanted her to do this on her own, to feel free. I didn't want to control her. But truth is, I wanted to watch her and make sure she was safe. I knew the cabin would be the perfect place. Considered telling her once she got here, you know? But then, I was afraid she wouldn't go, that she wouldn't leave me behind if she knew…I didn't want her to back out of the plans we had worked so hard to make. I wanted her to take the truck and go…to get away from him, and to protect her daughter. I love her, I really do…" Clara was crying again, choking sobs.

"So, you never talked to her in person or laid eyes on her?" I asked, aghast.

Clara shook her head but didn't look up.

"With all due respect, can you really love someone you've never actually met?"

Clara's head shot up, and she gave me a strange little smile. "I didn't need to see her face, Ellie. I'd already seen her soul."

We were quiet for several minutes, the only sound the rustling of the trees. Finally, I said, "You never answered my question earlier. Where is your husband now?"

Clara stared out at the barn, her eyes slanted. "In Florida with his mistress, just like I told Sam the other day. Good riddance to him. Wasn't as bad as Martin, but he caused just as much damage as he did."

I nodded, holding back more questions. My cell phone buzzed in my pocket.

"I need to see some of your messages with Nova." I said, resolutely.

"Absolutely," Clara said, tension draining from her face.

I plucked my phone from my pocket, reading new messages from Chad.

"Let me go get my phone. Be right back." As soon as she'd disappeared back inside, I stepped off the porch. Crossing the field, I made a beeline for the barn.

# CHAPTER FORTY-FOUR

*The Neighbor*

## CLARA

I emerged from my bedroom, phone in hand. Officer James was gone.

"Where'd you go?" I called, eyes traveling over the darkened field in terror.

Suddenly, from across the field, I heard the door to the barn slam shut. *She's going inside!*

Heart pounding, I raced through the muggy, marshy fields to stop her. *What will I do if she finds Andy? We had a plan—Nova and I—but then, Andy showed up and ruined everything! This was never part of the plan!*

When I stepped inside the barn, Officer James pointed her flashlight at me.

"Anything else you want to tell me, Clara?" Officer James asked. She was standing next to the old tractor, gripping her flashlight, thrusting it at me like a gun.

"No, of course not. I already told you everything I know."

Officer James shook her head. "No, I don't think that's true.

Rachel's dead. Nova's gone. Lily's missing…but that's not all, is it? Someone else is missing, too."

I took a step toward her, glancing nervously at the tractor. "I have no idea what you're talking about."

"Just like you had no idea who Nova was, *Al*."

I narrowed my eyes at her. *She knows. But how…?*

"I just got a message from one of my partners. We finally found a local who identified your husband's mistress. Her name is Rose Martin. Andy's not in Florida anymore. He left her. And guess where he told her he was headed…?"

I shrugged. What was the point? *Everything is coming unraveled…*

"Is your husband dead, too? Did you kill all of them, Clara?" Officer James asked. She squatted down beside the tractor, flashing her light underneath.

"That's my granddad's tractor. It hasn't been used in years…"

Officer James looked up at me and frowned. "The tractor's covered in dust. Even the floor around it is dusty. So, why does the floor underneath look so fresh, huh?"

Horrified, I watched as she squatted down and ran her hand across the floor. Finally, she stopped at the tiny notch where the false floor could be opened.

"There we go." She looked up at me, her face grim.

I sat down on the floor of the barn, my head spinning as I listened to her call for back-up.

# CHAPTER FORTY-FIVE

## *The Cop*

### ELLIE

"Where's Roland?" I stared at the cluster of officers and medical personnel on the scene. They were lifting Andy Appleton's decaying body from the cellar space beneath Clara Appleton's barn.

Clara had been taken away in handcuffs. Sergeant DelGrande was with her now. Considering his close relationship with her, I couldn't imagine how he was feeling right now…

"I don't know where he is. I think…still at the medical examiner's office. Waiting for the autopsy results for Rachel Coffey," Mike said.

Roland seemed to be the only one missing from this potential crime scene.

"Listen, Mike. I know you guys don't always trust me because of what happened with Ezra Clark…"

Mike shook his head and put up a hand to stop me. "You don't have to explain. We all knew he was a rotten drunk. But at one time, he was a good cop. And we just have this weird inclination to always protect our own…it could have happened to any of us. You did the right thing."

My eyebrows shot up. "Thank you," I said, awkwardly.

It felt good, hearing one of my fellow officers backing me up for once. I almost stopped myself from saying what I said next: "Listen, Mike. Roland knows more than he's saying. I'm not saying he was involved in Nova and Lily going missing, but he talked to her that night. For twenty-six minutes. Why wouldn't he tell us the truth?"

Mike chewed on his lips, eyes glazed and fuzzy, as he stared at the corpse being loaded into the back of the examiner's van.

"Mike. What aren't you guys telling me?"

Mike sighed and rubbed the back of his neck, feverishly.

"You can trust me, Mike. I'm listening. I just want to know…"

Mike turned to me and said, "It has nothing to do with Roland. He was drunk that night…too drunk to be handling the on-call line, too drunk to drive…so, I'm the one who took her call."

My eyes widened. "Mike! What did Nova say that night?"

"She wanted to know if we'd found her daughter. If we had any news. She was scared. I talked to her, tried to reassure her…"

"Okay…"

"And after I dropped off Roland, I decided I should ride by the cabin. Just in case. It was like three in the morning…"

"Mike. Did you go inside her cabin the night she went missing?" I asked, my pulse thudding in my ears. *Why didn't he tell me this earlier?!*

"No. It was the strangest thing…she was out on the road when I pulled up. Almost like…like, she'd been taking a late-night jog, or something. She got in the cruiser…and…I know this sounds crazy, but she was sweet. And scared. She asked if she could go back to my place."

"What?!" I stepped back from Mike, my eyes narrowing. *Did Mike do something to Nova?!*

As though he could hear my thoughts, he said, "I was a perfect gentleman, I swear. We talked. We had a few drinks at my place. We even watched a bit of a movie before the sun came up…but then I fell asleep. We didn't have sex…I didn't hurt her, I swear. When I woke up in the morning, she was gone. I don't even know how she got home, because I'd driven her to my place in my cruiser…and then I got called out to the cabin, and there was all this blood…"

"Mike. You have to tell this to Sergeant DelGrande. You can't hide this…why would you keep this a secret? You might have been the last person to see Nova Nesbitt alive."

"I was scared. I thought it'd get blamed on me, since I'd just been with her. It was unprofessional of me, taking her to my home…"

"Wait."

"What is it?" Mike asked.

"You said it was just Nova. But where was Lily? According to Clara, no one actually took her…it was all part of the plan to frame Martin, so they could get away…"

I looked back and forth, between Mike standing beside me and Clara's farmhouse.

*Either he was lying, or Clara was. One of them knew the truth…*

# CHAPTER FORTY-SIX

*The Mother*

*65 hours earlier…*

## NOVA

"He's a-asleep. L-listen, I d-didn't really have a ch-choice, Al. I-It was M-Martin…I saw him." I explained to her how I'd gotten into Officer Mike's cop car. He was a sweet man, just concerned about me and my missing daughter…

"I-I'm fine," I'd told him. "J-just focus on f-finding my daughter, pl-please…" I'd already talked to Al and I already knew she had her, but I had to play the part and I needed him to leave…

He had promised he would. He had promised to check up on me the next day. I got out of his cruiser, eager for him to pull away so that I could go back and get the bag and the truck…but that's when I saw him…*Martin.*

From the darkened windows of the cabin, like a ghoul looking out at me, he was watching me with the cop. He was waiting for me to come inside…waiting to kill me…

"Wait." I turned around, running after the policeman. I ran, hard as I could, chasing his taillights. The sound of his slamming brakes, was the sweetest sound in the world...

"Oh. I almost didn't see you...you okay?"

He opened his passenger door and I climbed back inside, shaking. "I'm fine. J-just s-scared that's all. I appreciate you checking on me. C-can we go somewhere for a little while... someplace safe? Will you take me home with you?" I'd asked him.

I had to wait for hours, until he fell asleep...as soon as I was sure he was snoring, I'd used his phone to call Al.

"C-can you c-come get me? Is Lily still safe with you?" I asked Al, my voice trembling.

"She's safe. She's exactly where I told her to stay. I saw Martin out there too. But he's gone now. For all he knows, I'm just an old lady, no one to worry about..."

"You s-saw him! Are you at the cabin?"

"I'm next door, Nova. I'm sorry I didn't tell you, I just thought you might change your mind...he snooped around and then he left. We're fine, I promise. She's hidden. We will come get you now. But I can't get in touch with Rachel though. I'm a little worried," Al said.

"I'm w-worried, too." I gave her the address, then waited on Mike's front porch for her to come and get me. I was going to see Al for the first time. She was taking me to her home, and Lily would be there too...together, we could get away from Martin for good. And hopefully, watch from the shadows while he went to prison for murder.

# CHAPTER FORTY-SEVEN

*The Cop*

## ELLIE

When Nova and Lily Nesbitt emerged from Clara's basement, it was like seeing two ghosts…I'd been so convinced that they would be dead and that one may not even exist…

Clara/Al had cleaned them out a neat little space in her basement. There were board games and books spread out on the floor. Two fluffy red sleeping bags…Nova was shocked when we found her, and angry about us taking her partner to jail. But she wasn't the same terrified woman that'd I met that first day. She didn't stutter; she stood tall, clutching the hand of the rosy-cheeked child beside her as we descended the stairs to the basement.

"It will all be okay, my love," Nova had promised her daughter. "These people just want to know that you're safe."

The blue-eyed beauty smiled up at me, timidly. Her words like whispers, she said, "I'm always safe with my Mama."

After the case was closed, I'd taken a three-week vacation. I'd just needed a break.

Now that I was back, my first order of business was to talk to

Sergeant DelGrande about our process for handling domestic violence cases in our county. I wanted to make sure that women like Nova didn't have to go to extraordinary lengths just to stay alive. And that women who were trying to help—like Rachel and Clara—could stay safe too.

I wanted to be a woman *and* a police officer. Pretty *and* tough. But I missed the point completely, until now. Because now I realize that working a certain job doesn't make me more of a man and painting up my face doesn't make me more of a woman. Being pretty doesn't change the way I do my job, and my job doesn't make me any less pretty. I'm just me, being my own version of what it means to be a confident woman, and I don't have to choose either/or anymore.

After finding Andy Appleton and unraveling the strange Nesbitt plot, my colleagues were treating me differently...slowly, but surely, I was becoming one of them. They were learning to trust me, and at the same time, I was starting to trust them too.

# CHAPTER FORTY-EIGHT

*The Neighbor*

## CLARA

By the time I made it to the forest, her body was gone. Hauled away, then tucked away until she could be poked and prodded after death. All I wanted to do was touch her. I wanted to say goodbye to my sister.

I heard they found her under a peach tree. There was more than one peach tree out there in those woods, but as soon as I saw it, I knew I'd found the right one. It was the biggest one, the spot where that monster dumped her body.

I know it sounds crazy, but as I crawled beneath that tree, scurrying into the shady darkness of the branches above, I thought I could feel her there.

The other night I had a dream, one of those dreams you can't dream twice. Rachel and I were sitting on the edge of a jagged cliff, dangling our toes over the side of Widow's Curve. "Now this is what you call living on the edge. Literally," Rachel giggled. She jumped from the edge before I could stop her.

She burst apart into tiny little particles before she hit the ground below.

Sometimes, I imagine those bits of her floating back into me, filling me up and making me whole again.

I made her a grave marker, similar to Annie's, and our sister Allison's. Now they lie side by side. I like to think that they're intertwined, whispering secrets beneath the dirt and soil...

The other day, I saw Martin on TV again. They were finally able to match his DNA to tiny bits of blood on the heel of my sister's sneakers. I like to think that even though she died, Rachel got to have the last laugh in the end. His clients who went house-hunting finally admitted that they were *occupied* during that timeframe and Martin could have left and killed her. There were also prostitutes who came forward, verifying that he was a violent man. And some of Lily's furniture and belongings were discovered at the local dump...

I think he'll be convicted, but you never know. I guess if he's not, I might have to take matters into my own hands, like I did with Andy.

Like the curl at the bend in Widow's Curve, Rachel was destined to die no matter which way she went. I only wish I could have saved her...but now, Nova and Lily will watch over her and the other ghosts on the farm while I'm gone. I stand trial next month for Andy's murder. I may have to serve some time, but there are a lot of people on my side—Officer James, Sergeant Sam, and even my husband's former mistress—and I've never felt freer. My lawyer will plead self-defense and hopefully, I'll get to spend the rest of my days with Nova and Lily, my new family.

As I stare at Nova's beautiful, smiling face, and as I watch Lily running freely through the fields...I know it was all worth it. I couldn't save my own daughter or my sister, but I have saved these two...and for now, that is enough.

# ACKNOWLEDGEMENTS

I owe a million thanks to Charlotte Ledger, Emily Ruston, and all of the staff at Killer Reads who helped make this book what it is today. The amount of work that went into this book is incredible. Charlotte and Emily, I don't know how you all manage to make my books look so good, but I am forever grateful for your magic. Keep sprinkling that fairy dust on my books, please!

I would also like to thank my agent, Katie Shea Boutillier, who helped me brainstorm ideas for this book and pushed me so hard to make each character really pop from the page. Without you, Katie, this book never would have happened. And together, we brought these ladies to life…

To my funny, intelligent, creative, beautiful, bull-headed daughter—Violet—I'm proud to be your mother. To my handsome, intelligent, caring sons—Tristian and Dexter—I'm so proud of the men you are becoming. And to my husband, Shannon, for supporting me every step of the way in my writing process and for being the best possible partner a girl could ask for.

To all of the readers, bloggers, and librarians—you all are the true champions of the book world, and I appreciate you taking a chance on my books.

Last but not least, to all of the women who have inspired me with your quiet strength and resilience over the years…you are the bravest warriors I know. And for those who are no longer with me…I will never forget.

# KILLER READS

## DISCOVER THE BEST
## IN CRIME AND THRILLER

**Follow us on social media to get to know the team behind the books, enter exclusive giveaways, learn about the latest competitions, hear from our authors, and lots more:**

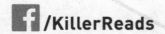 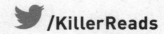